ROAD TO HELL

To Charles
Thanks for all
the times you kicked my
ass! I needed it
Kaija D Ball
Jan 2012

Published by Mundania Press
Also by Krista D. Ball

Tranquility's Blaze*

**Forthcoming*

ROAD TO HELL

KRISTA D. BALL

A Mundania Press Production
Mundania Press LLC
6457 Glenway Avenue, #109
Cincinnati, Ohio 45211-5222

To order additional copies of this book, contact:
books@mundania.com
www.mundania.com

Edited by Adruenne Jones

Trade Paperback ISBN: 978-1-60659-287-8
eBook ISBN: 978-1-60659-286-1

First Edition • December 2011

Production by Mundania Press LLC
Printed in the United States of America

10 9 8 7 6 5 4 3 2 1

DEDICATION

To Michael and Jacob, who were grounded at a lot during the writing of this book. Sorry guys.

CHAPTER ONE

"This is the worst alcohol I've ever tasted."

Katherine smirked at the way John, one of her oldest friends and current second-in-command, wrinkled his nose after finishing his tall glass of homemade port. "Want me to pour you another one?"

"Please," he said. Everyone laughed, including Katherine who took his glass and walked to the tiny kitchenette on the far side of her quarters. After topping up his drink, she popped her head around the corner and shouted out, "Anyone else want a refill?"

The other two women in the room, Bindu Raewadee and Lori Windrunner, both fervently shook their heads. Katherine didn't blame them. The port had the consistency of gravy. She poured another generous serving and headed back to the living area.

"Thanks, Katherine," John said, accepting the drink.

Katherine slid down the wall to settle cross-legged on the floor. Her three senior officers, the ones not currently working in Operations, sat scrunched together on her tiny sofa, the only piece of proper sitting furniture she owned, beyond a desk chair. She sat across from them, her back cooled by the unfinished, metal wall. She picked up her plate of reconstituted spaghetti and soy meatballs from the coffee table. If the port tasted like conduit fluid, the pasta tasted like conduit foam.

John raised the glass to his lips and guzzled the viscous

liquid, all eyes on him. He shook his head, frowning. "Lori, this is disgusting."

Lori put on her best injured face. A good one, too, in Katherine's opinion. "You asked me, *Commander Roberts*, to provide you with a steady stream of non-corrosive alcohol. It is not my fault that it tastes like single malt from the Scottish Highlands." She gave an indignant sniff.

John narrowed his eyes and, with his best Scottish brogue, growled, "Do not mock the Highlands."

Katherine laughed and looked at Perdition Docking Port's newest head of engineering, Second Lieutenant Bindu Raewadee. Why they sent her a puppy straight out of school to head up repairs on an entire port was beyond her. The kid seemed bright enough at least, if a little too shy. "Ignore them. They've been in space too long. We're seeing the first signs of space dementia."

Bindu offered a tense smile. She looked at her full glass of port and back at Katherine. "It really does look like conduit fluid."

The ceiling pipes clanged, shaking the walls and floor. All Perdition's senior staff snapped their heads up and toward the eardrum-crushing sound, except for Katherine. After three months of living in the make-shift quarters, she barely noticed when her neighbors one deck up flushed their toilets. Instead, she stayed focused on twisting the barely-edible noodles around her fork, which proved significantly more difficult than it should have.

"God, Katherine. How much longer will you have to live here?" John asked.

"Engineering," she said, half-heartedly glaring at Bindu, who visibly flinched, "promises my old quarters will be habitable again within the month."

John scoffed. "What's the point of being the captain of a space port if you can't even get your own bedroom fixed?"

"Damned if I know."

They shared a laugh, and Katherine took a deep breath,

soaking in the moment. Twenty minutes into supper, and the war had still not been mentioned. No doubt it was still there, weighing on their minds. It would be impossible for it not to plague them, considering where they were eating. Her quarters, once along the outer ring with a great view of Dock Five, now existed in a converted cargo bay. The old apartment sat unrepaired after the Coalition attack on Perdition three months before, which left a significant portion of the habitat ring unsafe.

At least for now, the black cloud of war had not penetrated dinner. For that, she gave silent thanks.

"One of these days, I'd like to visit my old quarters without needing a zero-grav suit," Katherine said, her tone gruff, though she did wear a smile.

"I'm not sure your quarters will be finished on time," Bindu said, clearing her throat, and she pulled out a hand-sized silver data device from her satchel of tools which sat on the floor. "I received this message before I arrived, Captain, err Katherine."

Katherine opted not to mention the mistake of using rank during Sunday dinner. She remembered what it was like trying to balance the job with after hours, having once been a young officer a lifetime ago. As it was, she struggled to think of her as "Bindu," even when off-duty. John and Lori were different; they were old friends. But, apparently, personal interaction with the troops was important, according to Dr. Adam Win, Jr. of Earth, and who was she to argue with a man possessing initials both before and after his name?

"New orders to delay having my old room back, huh? Let me see them." She leaned closer to take the pad from the young woman and froze. She stared at the thick, brown goo in Bindu's bowl. "What *is* that?"

Bindu looked down at her food and back up to Katherine. "The package said lentil soup."

John leaned over Lori to stare at the soup. He frowned. "Mental note. Avoid the lentil soup. You'd think they'd have come up with decent emergency rations by now."

Katherine gave John an exaggerated roll of her eyes, mostly

for the benefit of her new head of engineering. He did have a valid point, however. What she would give for fresh fruit! Coalition ships had destroyed the last two convoys destined to resupply Perdition. Ajax, the planet that Perdition orbited, lost most of its agricultural lands in the penultimate Coalition attack and now lacked enough food to export. Until the convoys got through, all Fleet personnel ate emergency rations, so that the civilians could be allotted whatever fresh food the docking port still had in storage or managed to produce on the hydroponics level.

Katherine nodded at the data pad and then gave Bindu a pointed look, waiting for her to hand over the new orders she'd received.

"Oh, it's an update from the Corps. They're ordering all in-dock ships to be retrofitted with triple nanite-fibre barriers and an independent blast system at each junction point. No one can leave for the front without it. Also, the Tenth Fleet has been ordered to Perdition, so that we can upgrade their ships. They'll arrive in thirteen days."

The entire Tenth Fleet? Katherine did not like the sound of that.

Katherine's voice turned firm, switching easily into the tone she reserved for her role of captain. "Lieutenant Raewadee," she began, "this is a major project. To implement it, the entire engineering team will need to be pulled off shield maintenance, not to mention repairing the last of the internal damage. Why is this the first I've heard of it?"

A rosy flush spread across Raewadee's dark features. She spoke fast, as Katherine observed she often did when nervous. "The message came in on my way here, so I downloaded it while I was walking." She handed the pad to Katherine. "I haven't even read the entire order yet. I thought it would be best to stay for a bit, since our Sunday dinners, well, are important. I'm sorry. I didn't realize—"

Katherine held up a silencing hand. "No major harm done. Next time, let us know that something important has come up.

While we don't generally talk shop during dinner, we can make exceptions for major overhauls like this." A learning opportunity was still a learning opportunity, even when it happened over a meal of reconstituted food.

The room fell silent as Katherine scanned the document. Technical data well beyond her skill level filled most of it. She was about to hand the pad back when the communications panel chirped.

"Incoming message from Ensign Ostyn."

She gave everyone an apologetic look. Needing to stretch her legs, she opted to walk to the communications panel instead of using voice command. Using the panel would bypass having the call piped through her quarters, too. She tapped the blinking red square in the middle of the screen. "Francis here."

"Captain, I apologize for bothering your dinner," said a frantic feminine voice through the speaker. "It's only that news came in from one of the trader vessels, and we can't—"

"Ensign Ostyn! Spill it," Katherine snapped.

The caller gulped and spoke slower, though the shake hadn't left her voice. "A merchant convoy entered communications range."

Katherine nodded. Perhaps this was the overdue grocery run. Anything to move away from emergency rations.

"Captain Baker of the *Pharaoh* said the Coalition captured Pious III last week."

The hairs on the back of her neck stood on end and a cold chill gripped her body.

Home.

Her breath hitched in her throat. She swallowed hard to move the rising lump that threatened to cut off her air supply. Once certain that tears would not fall, she looked over her shoulder. John was already at her side, his expression concerned but hard. The room tilted on its axis for a moment, and her heart pounded out of control.

Eighteen years of service prepared her for war. It did not prepare her for the invasion of her home planet.

"Are you certain that's what he said?" Her voice cracked, but she forced out a long breath. The technique calmed her enough to focus on the ensign's words, though not enough to stop her pounding heart.

"Yes, Captain. Since he didn't witness it himself, I've sent a message to Sector Command for confirmation."

"That was quick thinking. Good job." Katherine nodded, even if the woman couldn't see her; vid-mode was not generally used on the docking port to conserve power. Obtaining confirmation would not have occurred to most ensigns. "We'll be right there."

She tapped the screen again, ending the transmission. Even though she was in the company of friends, they were also her subordinates. Pushing aside her grief came with the job. She sucked in a lungful of air and expelled it forcefully. "Dinner's over."

Lori stared at her, pale and wide-eyed, but nodded. Katherine turned to Raewadee. Small rivulets of tears trickled down the younger woman's dark face, and Lori put a supportive hand on Raewadee's shoulder.

Katherine wanted to offer a supportive smile, but she didn't have the strength. With only a month on Perdition and straight out of university, Raewadee hadn't developed a thick skin for death yet. Katherine gave her credit, though. The young woman sniffled and quivered but held back the rest of her tears. Katherine had more practice keeping the outward mask, but that did not mean the grief didn't touch her. It did and shook the marrow in her bones.

Thankfully, John was there, offering age and experience for her to mirror. Katherine didn't know a harder man than John, and she yearned to be surrounded by that cold detachment to keep her own emotions in check. If the attack were true, her family was already dead. The Coalition rarely left survivors. She pushed the thought aside and focused on her next steps.

John narrowed his eyes at her. "You ready?"

Katherine nodded, her gaze lingering on a palm-sized

photo stream hanging on the wall. Pictures of her last visit home, of her sister and step-mother, faded in and out. She pressed together her lips, fighting rage and fear. She tapped the door panel. It hissed opened, and she hurried to OPs, her senior officers behind her, boots clacking against the metal floor.

Silently, she begged the universe to let it be just another rumor. Her gut told her otherwise.

CHAPTER TWO

Fourteen hours and six shuttle-craft-sized cups of burned coffee later, the confirmation arrived.

"Incoming message on Fleet Emergency Channel, Captain," said a male over the speaker on her computer console. Katherine didn't recognize his voice, but he sounded young enough to be one of the new officers working in OPs to help with less critical tasks. There were so many these days, she couldn't keep track anymore.

"Put it through."

The 3D holo-vid projector clicked. A blur of color appeared for a brief moment before clearing. A quarter-meter tall image of an older female in a black pantsuit displayed upward from the palm-sized projection disk on her desk. Katherine held her breath.

"We regret to inform the citizens of the Union of Planets that Pious III, one of our most remote geological research stations, was captured by the Coalition. The last transmission from the planet was June 19 2723 CE, eleven a.m. local time confirming the Coalition invasion force had broken through planetary defenses. The Union Parliament sends its condolences to the families of those who were lost or are still missing."

The muscles of Katherine's back tensed and part of her longed to curl into a ball of grief. A larger part seethed in anger. She grabbed on to that aspect of her pain and held it tight, massaged it, coerced it to grow. No doubt, the brass hats sitting in Fleet Command thought withholding news of the Coalition's invasion would be good for morale. They had not considered that merchant captains couldn't keep a fart to themselves, let alone the conquering of a planet.

The matronly politician in the video message finished reading the sterilized details of the invasion, her eyes grim.

"The Union Parliament sends its thanks to all the brave Fleet soldiers who risk their lives every day for our freedom. We particularly wish to recognize and honor the sacrifices made by those citizens who are settled near the Coalition borders, who continue to work and live even with the threat of war so close to their homes.

"Rest assured that the Union Parliament is doing everything it can to stop the conflict."

Katherine rolled her eyes as the woman's 3D image faded away. "Inbred politicians." Parliament most certainly was *not* doing everything possible.

An alphabetized list of the dead, injured, and missing appeared on Katherine's main console, cutting off her one-sided argument with the unnamed politician.

She watched the names with cold detachment. At least, she started to. The flute rendition of "Danny Boy" floated into audible range. Her jaw clenched. Damn. That had been her father's favorite song.

Thank God he didn't live to see this.

She watched the white-text names against the black background. The Dead. The Injured. The Missing. Or, as popular talk called it, the "Dead, Dying, and Probably Dead" list.

Katherine flinched and chided herself for letting those words seep into her mind. She had a standing order that any soldier caught uttering that particular phrase was to receive a double duty rotation in sanitation. The assumption unaccounted-for people were already dead was downright offensive to Perdition civilians who still waited for news of their loved ones. It was demoralizing for the Fleet troops who had lost friends.

Yet, the phrase played over and over in her mind, like a broken music stream. With the Coalition, the saying was true. There wouldn't be survivors. There were never survivors.

No tears came though, even as the names of her friends and family scrolled on the screen. Instead, near-blinding rage formed a tornado in her gut. She gritted her teeth against the storm, her body shaking.

Sherry Terrance, Missing in Action.

Katherine's math teacher in high school. She had never quite forgiven Ms. Terrance for that failing grade on a group assignment.

She clenched her fists and snarled.

Jesse Meyerson. Missing in Action.

Jesse and Katherine lost their virginity together in the crystal caverns outside the colony. The only man she had ever slept with. Gone.

Grief tightened its grip on her throat.

Alysha Francis. Confirmed dead.

A gasp escaped Katherine.

Her baby sister worked at an outer ring hospital. She must have been home for a visit. Rage rattled Katherine's spine, sending chills throughout her body. The urge to scream, hit, smash threatened to overwhelm nearly two decades of training.

Judith Haise. Confirmed dead.

Her stepmother and last remaining parent. Gone.

Heat rose inside her. Fuming anger swelled. They had invaded her home. They had killed her loved ones.

They were going to pay.

"Murderous sons of bitches," Katherine growled as she grasped the edge of her desk, talking herself down from destroying...it didn't matter what, so long as she could crush something. The more she read, the more her mind filled with blood-thirsty thoughts, fantasies of wrapping her bare hands around the neck of anyone associated with the Coalition and squeezing until bones cracked. She wanted to do to them what they'd no doubt done to her family.

No.

She wanted to do worse than anything they'd done. She didn't care that the Coalition were humans. They were animals in her eyes. Animals meant for slaughter. And they'd fucking killed her family.

Katherine grabbed her stainless steel coffee cup and slammed it into the console panel that jutted from her desk at a comfortable reading angle. The cup and her hand smashed through the protective barrier, cracking the panel underneath. Sparks flared and wires puffed out a breath of smoke. Plastic-coated safety glass pebbled around her hand and embedded itself into her skin. She shook from the anger, ignoring the tiny drops of blood on her pale flesh and the burning sting of tiny lacerations.

She took several deep breaths, hoping to cool the boiling emotions down to a manageable level. She had a senior officers' meeting to attend. They needed to be shown the message and filled in on the details before the announcement on the docking port's communications Net could be posted.

Protocol during wartime had to be followed. Anger had to be managed.

A full minute passed before Katherine gained enough control to stand up from her desk, neat and organized, except for the tiny shards of glass that gleamed against the black finish. She took the several steps to her transparent dual doors which whooshed open when she tapped the side panel.

Muted voices, beeps, and chimes filled the air. Katherine stepped out into the Operations Center, the heart of Perdition. She lifted her gaze up at the two upper levels before dropping it to the main floor of OPs. Her family was dead. She repeated it several times, allowing the coldness of the words to harden her grief.

Duty called.

Before heading toward the lift, she turned to a blond, young man. Another ensign whose name she didn't know. "Have the comm panel on my desk fixed."

CHAPTER THREE

Katherine stood off to the side of the metal, rectangular table as the official Pious III announcement played on a large projection monitor built into the wall. In front of her sat five of the officers who currently made up her senior staff, their expressions bleak. She would have preferred the entire team to be present, but two of her officers, medical sciences and personnel, were off-port at a conference.

"Monsters," Windrunner growled under her breath.

Katherine was unable to argue the point. Sweat pooled along the waistband of her uniform trousers. The environmental controls had broken the moment Raewadee pulled all engineers off port repairs to work on upgrading Perdition's extensive conduit system, along with every ship docked in port.

Murphy's Law of Space Docks: when it rains, everything breaks down.

The first few notes of "Danny Boy" broke the silence of the room. Katherine tapped the bottom right of the screen, as the names began their march across the black background. The feed ended, returning the screen to its glossy, black finish. Displaying the names during the meeting amounted to a waste of valuable time. The message would be on every screen on Perdition within the hour anyway. Her staff could read it then.

She allowed a moment of silence for her crew to collect themselves. It didn't matter that they weren't from Pious. What mattered was that it had happened. The silence also gave her a final opportunity to turn the last of her raw emotions to stone. Her crew needed her. All Perdition needed her. Her family and friends were already gone. She held no illusions of false hope. Nearly two decades of service had taught her that. Three years of brutal war taught her that. Those people were gone and would never be coming back.

"Any questions?" Katherine asked, scanning the faces of her officers, faces that were etched with every possible combination of grief and rage.

Commander Nova Ambrose, Perdition's head of security, raised her hand, exposing a sweat stain on her grey uniform. "How did they defeat the planet's defenses so quickly? Pious III is remote, but it had forty ships patrolling the area."

"There was a fragmented communication from the fleet there." Katherine looked down at the large console screen built into the table and flipped through the various digital folders for the information. Getting the details correct was important at any time but especially now. Her family deserved at least that. "The lead warship, ah the *Congo,* managed to transmit a garbled message to Sector Command before being destroyed. It appears the Coalition found a fault in our conduit construction on Class Four warships."

Whispers hissed through the room, but no one spoke up with a new question or comment. Katherine continued scanning the information. The number of sections and tabs steadily increased, and she couldn't keep up with the barrage of new material. She looked up at the group. "Raw data is still being transferred. We won't have any complete answers for several hours, perhaps even days. However, it does look like the Coalition fleet destroyed the *Congo* in less than two minutes. The rest of the patrol fell shortly after that." She left off the fact that there were no survivors. Salt did not need to be rubbed into that particular wound.

Lieutenant Commander Jayson Williams, head of tactical, shook his bald head. "I can't believe they took out a warship in two minutes. How fast until we can get the upgrades done?"

Raewadee shrugged and said, “Quite a while yet. We’re down an industrial processor as it is. To do this, we’d need to replace the broken one and find another one besides. We have three cargo bays of scrap metal plus eighteen ships in tow to be stripped. We can’t go any faster until we can melt down the scrap and manufacture the parts we need.”

Katherine drummed her fingers on the table. “All right, set aside five entry-level engineers dedicated to general maintenance and repairs.” She used her tunic sleeve to mop the sweat from her brow. “Tell them to start with climate control. It must be thirty-five degrees in here.”

She opened a text field to transmit a port-wide message to in-dock ships. “I’m requesting all ships to give us access to their onboard processors. We can use them to reprocess the smaller scrap and fabricate wiring and micro parts. Perdition can focus on the large items. Will that speed things along?”

“Yes, Captain, though I requested that yesterday. Only four ships accepted. The others felt it put undue strain on their ships.”

“Which ships agreed?”

Raewadee looked down at her own pad. “*Druid*, *Jane Austen*, *Terra Firma*, and *Wellington*.”

Katherine thought for a moment before typing in an addition to the message for the ships. “I’m adding the following: Upgrades will be placed on a first-to-volunteer, first-to-be-upgraded basis. Since those four—I’ve listed the ship names—granted us access, they will be placed at the front of the pack.” She tapped send and looked up. “That should make your life easier.”

“Thank you, Captain,” Raewadee said. A tiny smile formed, contrasting with the exhaustion in her eyes.

Katherine inclined her head; Raewadee’s smile was balm for her frayed emotions. At least she could do one thing today to make life a touch smoother for someone.

“Captain, so let me get this straight,” Windrunner said through clenched teeth. “Fleet Command knew about Pious

III when they sent Raewadee the upgrades list."

Katherine's spine went rigid. She nodded, though she gave a warning stare. Her patience was raw. They still had to speak to their individual departments to prepare them before she could post the message for public viewing. A lot of work had to be done. Whining wouldn't get it done.

Roberts sneered. "The patrol wasn't blown up because of a conduit fault, Windrunner, and you know it. They were destroyed because the Coalition was hiding in Alliance territory, crossed over, and surprised our ships."

"It's not like it hasn't happened before," Ambrose snapped back, nodding in agreement. "Pious III's protection fleet should have been prepared for it."

Frustration filled Katherine, though she wasn't certain if it was because of John's attitude or because Ambrose was right. She paused long enough to ensure her tone could remain calm before speaking. "I realize that it's unavoidable for the discussion to fall back to strategy, but let's avoid it today. We have a lot of work to do."

"Why shouldn't we discuss it?" Roberts asked. She could see the sweat beading on his face. "Everyone in this room knows the Neutrality Agreement between the Alliance and the Coalition is the real reason Pious III was captured. Unprotected conduits built too close to a ship's hull only sped things up."

Katherine licked her lips, trying to balance her own personal wish to fall into the negativity of blame against the need for duty and order. The room's stifling air didn't help. The stench of body odor pressed against her, along with the unrelenting stagnant air. It made her grief harder to manage.

She blew out a long breath. Perhaps addressing their feelings would be better than keeping them bottled up. "I know that the Agreement puts us at a disadvantage. We can't go into Alliance space to attack the Coalition, but they can use Alliance space to attack us. And, yes, it is frustrating when the Coalition is able to use Alliance border systems to hide from our scans. And, yes, it is frustrating that the Ethics Laws prevent us from using drone weaponry along the Alliance border."

Katherine threw back her shoulders and looked at the grim faces around her. "So we will work within the rules laid out by the Union's government."

Roberts muttered, "As long as the Neutrality Agreement exists and the bloody politicians make us follow the Ethics Laws to the letter, we'll lose this war to the Crazy Patrol."

All eyes stared at Katherine. She frowned, knowing she needed to address John's words, even if giving dignity to them was the last thing she wanted to do. She skimmed the console in front of her. Eight new sections had been added. She opened a new folder and scanned.

"The Coalition fleet," she drawled out, refusing to apply the "Crazy Patrol" nickname to them—they deserved no such attention—"approached Pious III from the Alliance boundary. Our ships hadn't been concentrating their patrols in that area and didn't notice the invasion fleet until it was too late. The planet's defenses were no match without the patrol to assist them."

Silence blanketed the room once more. Katherine found reading out the dry and neat facts of war easier to deal with than her grief. There was comfort in facts, like a warm blanket in winter.

"Intel reports six privately-owned ships, merchants and the like, one mining ship, who dropped its load to make room, and three survey ships escaped with approximately a thousand people. So, about a tenth of the colony's population." Her tone turned grim. "At least some were able to outrun them."

A small voice whispered its hope that some of her extended family and friends made it out and were merely missing from the refugee list. She shot the hope down. Katherine lacked the time for fantasies.

Roberts snorted, slamming his glass of water down hard on the steel table. Water sloshed over the sides, and he used the sleeve of his grey uniform to clean it up. "Our weapons are shit against Coalition shields, but at least Fleet engines are the best in the galaxy. We can outrun anyone, any place, any time." He gave a sloppy salute, his thumb crossing his open palm.

"That's enough, Commander," Katherine shouted far louder than she had planned. Heat rose in her face. She leaned forward, hands on the table, and took control of her tone. "If you are going to be sarcastic and salute, please do it correctly with your palm facing open and flat, your fingers tight, and your thumb parallel with your hand. Otherwise, I suggest you continue to show the proper respect worthy of your rank."

He gave her a weak, but apologetic, smile. "Yes, Captain. I'm sorry. I'm just...*tired*."

"We're all tired." She sucked in a breath of stale, hot air. "Look, I agree with all of you. The Alliance's neutrality and blind eye is making everything more difficult on us. However, losing people is expected during wartime."

Katherine's voice hitched uncontrollably. She took a sip of water and swallowed hard, hoping to disguise the momentary lapse as thirst. Not that her crew would care. It was her pride that would. "I realize that it's upsetting and demoralizing. But that doesn't mean we're losing the war."

Windrunner scoffed, her light brown skin almost pink from either frustration or the rising heat in the room. Katherine figured most likely both. "Were you in the same meeting as the rest of us yesterday? Intel says we have a thirty-seven percent chance of winning the war. In my eyes, that means we're losing right now."

Katherine kept her tone calm. She had lost more than anyone else in that room. They needed to see her calm in the face of her grief, even if they didn't know it. If she could remain in control, so could they. "Fleet Command has requested that all captains and higher provide a local action plan to help bring about a faster end to the war. If you come up with any suggestions, no matter how small, I want you to let me know."

A sour laugh escaped Roberts. "Short of the Alliance joining our side, we're screwed."

"The Alliance isn't going to join our side. They have their

damned Neutrality Agreement. They pretend not to take sides in the conflict, all the while letting the Coalition inside their borders to attack us," Ambrose said, shaking her head, blond curls bouncing.

Katherine decided it was time to end the meeting. They'd had their moment to complain and feel that they were in charge. Time to work now. "I don't plan to start singing, 'Hail the Conquerors' yet, and none of you should, either. So, let's brave up and put on our best faces. Civilians don't want to see us falling apart. We have a long day ahead of us. Let's get on with it. Dismissed."

The group came to their feet, chair joints squeaking. Feet scuffed against the carpet. As the staff shuffled out, they whispered quietly amongst themselves. Katherine avoided meeting anyone's eyes. Glances of sympathy would not help her.

"Commander Roberts, a word," she said, not looking up.

He walked over to her. When the door closed behind the last officer, he said, "I'm sorry, Katherine."

"You should be." She straightened herself and looked up at him to meet his gaze. Katherine was a tall woman, but next to him, she felt tiny. "John, you're my second in command. I expect a better attitude from you, especially today of all days." Her voice quavered for a moment before taking control again.

The dark circles around his eyes and his snow white hair made him seem decades older than his mere forty-six years. "I'm sorry about your home."

His words tore at her walls. She lifted a hand. "I'm not ready."

John nodded at her, his eyes filled with understanding. "I have a department to speak to. We can have dinner later, okay? I'll bring the Scotch."

Katherine forced a half-hearted smile and nodded. She waited for the doors to swoosh closed behind him. Tears stung her eyes, but she held them back.

John was right about one thing. The Ethics Laws crippled their defensive abilities. Katherine had often thought a drone system of sorts could be installed along the Alliance borders to signal whenever Coalition ships crossed over. Even a minute's extra warning could be enough to save millions of lives. Of course, it went against the spirit of the Union's government, who refused to have any form of aggressive technology along their borders.

A dangerous thought crossed her mind. They had been losing because of their strict adherence to the Ethics Laws. The Coalition didn't hold the same sorts of morals sacred the way the Union did. Perhaps, a minor greying of a few rules could help.

She took a deep breath. She knew exactly what to do.

CHAPTER FOUR

After her senior officers' meeting, she made a few key visits to different departments to provide a boost to morale. They needed to see her in control and uncompromised. Unfortunately, it also put her in the midst of Perdition's grief as the official announcement regarding Pious III played on the public screens.

Uncomfortably damp from the sweat and rainforest humidity, Katherine arrived at her office through the back entrance, opting to circumvent going through OPs and its barrage of chatter, reports, and distractions. She needed to stay focused.

She tapped the communications link on her desk console. A young man appeared on the vid screen a moment later, his curly red hair resembling an emergency evac light. She made a mental note to remind him to not use vid chat; it drained an unnecessary amount of power. "Oh, hi Captain. I didn't know you were in your office. What can I do for you?"

She made an additional note to have someone train him on proper communications protocol. Did they teach the new kids anything these days?

It took Katherine a couple of seconds to remember his name. Too many new people. So many gone. "O'Connor, I need a secure channel opened to Admiral Samantha Ortora at Command Headquarters."

O'Connor nodded briskly. "It'll take me a bit to work it out. It's—" the computer chirped as his fingers tapped several buttons on the touch-screen monitor "—the middle of the night in South Africa right now, so she might not answer for several hours."

"Flag it as highest priority. Put in the message, 'Tokyo.' That'll get her out of bed."

His brows drew together. "Yes, Captain. I'll signal you when she's online."

Katherine terminated the transmission line. Waiting. Little else frustrated her as much as time that stretched out for eternity whenever she had to wait for something or someone. Her muscles clenched as she ran through different scenarios in her mind. She needed to keep her mind on target.

She was about ask Admiral Ortora for permission to grey the Ethics Laws.

Her mouth went dry. The conversation would go one of two ways. Sam would either lean toward her thinking, or spend an hour lecturing her. She had to try, though.

Katherine stared at the blinking number on the corner of her screen. Over a hundred unread messages waited for her. Since she had no idea how long it would take to establish a secure channel opened to Earth—the security protocols changed hourly—Katherine opted to sift through the internal reports that filled her inbox.

She skimmed the repair reports, one concerning ship upgrades and the other outlining Perdition's upkeep.

Katherine tapped the screen and made a few modifications to the upkeep list—non-critical items like establishing basic computer access for the bulk of the civilian population who lacked it. Returning computer access to the civilian population was essential for morale and a good practice project for the five new engineers that Raewadee assigned to repairs.

Engineering had been putting off computer access issues, as stable gravity and atmosphere were more important. Now that these were fixed, computers and environmental controls were next.

A previous Coalition attack, the one that sent her quarters into space, had taken out part of the habitat section, leaving many civilians and lower-ranking personnel without working consoles in their makeshift quarters in the cargo bays. Major announcements had to be made on the projection screens in the common areas, once used for advertisements, news, and docking information.

Today, those screens broadcasted the names of the dead from Pious III.

In an ideal universe, the upload would have been available only for private viewing. Ideal situations didn't exist in wartime. So, a public announcement was all she could do. Getting private computer access set up would allow future announcements to have more dignity, being uploaded in private. Allowing private grief.

Future announcements. Katherine pushed aside the tugging emotions. She could not afford to grieve. The cold exterior of command had to stay in place. The connection with Earth could be established at any moment; beginning the call in tears would be less than professional. Repairs and upgrades needed to be monitored. The Tenth Fleet would arrive soon.

She was too damned busy to grieve.

Katherine skipped over condolence messages from Sister Mary Nora, Iman Arash, and Priestess Barbara, forwarding them to her personal storage folder. When she was ready, she'd read them. It wasn't that she was opposed to the religious folks—she was a quasi-practicing Catholic, after all—but she did not want to be prayed for or blessed. She didn't want to talk about her feelings, or have prayers uttered, requesting soothing balms for her soul.

She also declined a meeting request from the counseling center. If she couldn't handle priests, she certainly couldn't handle being psychoanalyzed by children fresh out of shrink school. They'd eventually force the issue, but Katherine could play difficult for at least a month. By then, she'd have processed everything and would be in the frame of mind to talk. At least, enough to satisfy Fleet Mental Health that she wasn't going to crack and start weeping in the halls.

The ceiling vent creaked. Frigid air slammed against Katherine's sweat-soaked uniform. She sighed. The environmental system had to get fixed and soon. Space ports should never have a cold front passing through.

She buzzed O'Connor again. "Ensign, what's the status on the line?"

He obviously had vid mode turned on automatic because her screen filled with his red mop. The air filled with a number of "ums" and "ahhs." "The message hasn't made it to the Saturn Relay Station yet, Captain."

"What's taking so long?" she demanded.

"Um, we lost two communications relays last week, and Sector Engineering Corps hasn't been able to replace them yet."

Katherine sighed but nodded. She had a vague recollection of an Intel report mentioning that. Too much happening in too little time. Events had started to merge and twist together.

"I'll let you know as soon as it's open."

She wasn't a supporter of ensigns in command, but there were barely enough troops to send into combat, let alone help run the many stations and ports throughout Union space. It wasn't that she didn't like him. O'Connor wasn't a bad soldier for being three months out of UFU. Still, he was barely nineteen. She didn't want children to die for ethics or morals anymore. She wanted the dying to stop.

The Admiral had requested ideas to end the war. She had one.

She tapped her computer's voice command icon. "Computer, display a map of the highest occurrences of Coalition attacks against Union ships and territory. Limit to those within a parsec of Alliance space and within this sector only."

"Working," the computer's masculine voice replied. A multi-colored spiral spun around the screen as the computer worked to bring up the visual of what she'd requested.

Her plan for Ortora was still vague, but Katherine felt it hit the heart of the issue. Discover what latitude existed in bending the Ethics Laws. The inherent passivity of the Union of Planets had made them appear weak to the Coalition. Like any good predator, they began culling the galactic herd. Now three years into the war, Katherine agreed that the Union was indeed weak. With a population adverse to conflict, they had not been prepared for a full-scale invasion.

"Inquiry completed. Identify flat or 3D."

"3D."

A meter-high three-dimensional image appeared over the middle of her desk, emanating from the small, glossy-black circle next to her display monitor. "Computer, highlight the Union/Alliance border in yellow."

A fluorescent yellow line, weaving and dipping, divided the territories represented. The image slowly rotated. Small white lights blinked along the yellow line, the border. Eight large clumps of white lights signaled the areas of highest Coalition attacks next to the Alliance border.

She examined the attack points with cold detachment. "Computer, highlight in green where the Alliance's communication jamming is the strongest."

Katherine already knew that the green would appear where the white lights flashed. The Coalition used the Alliance's defensive border as a shield to attack the Union. She'd seen it in countless reports already.

Katherine stared at the rotating image, its flashing white area surrounded by a green hue. She pondered her options against the Ethics Laws. They weren't military law; they were governmental law which was far worse. Even during wartime, some would say especially during wartime, the civilian government would figuratively crucify any military personnel violating the Ethics Laws.

Katherine accepted their usefulness most days. The Ethics Laws allowed civilians living in the core sector, untouched by war, to feel self-righteous in their refusal to lower themselves to barbarism and cruelty. The problem was that they were losing the war, even though the news media sure made it sound different. Unchecked, the Union's self-righteous hubris would have them turned into the galaxy's slave race within a decade.

Unless she did something about it.

Biogenetic weapons, drone weapon platforms, and space mines were off the table. Command had also resisted automated defense drones along the borders in the past because aggressive movements in peacetime were against the Ethics Laws.

It wasn't peacetime anymore. If Katherine could convince Ortora to let her people create stealth communications drones, they could, at least, transmit messages through the interference of the area. Nearby ships and planets could be put on alert if a Coalition ship was detected crossing the Alliance's borders into Union space. Those precious seconds could be enough to allow evacuation ships to activate their jump drives and escape.

Katherine nodded to herself, approving of her plan. She stared at the computer visual for a moment longer before the communications panel buzzed.

"Captain, I have Admiral Ortora for you. She's requested vid chat," Ensign O'Connor said.

"Go ahead," Katherine said, smoothing down the front of her uniform, the fabric damp from sweat and cold from the over-active air conditioning.

The monitor blinked. A grainy image appeared on the screen. It took Katherine's eyes a moment to adjust. A middle-aged woman, still in her pink nightgown, yawned. The background was dark. Ortora hadn't bothered turning the lights on.

"Katherine," she said, not bothering to hide her annoyance, "this better be important."

"It is, Sam." Katherine smiled at her old UFU friend. "Remember when I bailed you out of that Tokyo drunk tank and didn't tell anybody?"

The Admiral snorted.

"I'm calling in the favor."

The smile faded. "What do you need?" Ortora's voice was choppy and delayed, the prime indicator that the secure channel was working. The ensign had done a good job.

Katherine hoped that their decades-long friendship would

not fail her. She took a deep breath. "You asked for ideas on how to end the war. How much leeway can you give me in the Ethics Laws?"

Ortora raised her eyebrows. "Are you certain this line is secure?"

Katherine blinked at that. "My end is."

"Hold on for a moment." Ortora reached her arm out, presumably to touch the wall panel, and the screen went blank.

Confused, Katherine stared at the black screen. She had not expected Sam to put her on hold to confirm the security connection. Normally, the confirmation of one side was good enough. Katherine shrugged it off as wartime paranoia and worked on her sales pitch.

Perdition Docking Port was on the outer rim and a layover point for ships leaving for and retreating from the front. They were in a perfect location to make the stealth drones and distribute them throughout the sector. Perdition already manufactured repair drones as needed for ships returning to the front. Making stealth drones would be trickier but doable.

A drone could pick up an enemy ship and bombard Union communications on all frequencies faster and easier than a ship could. Also, the drones could be programmed to deploy message probes to get the alerts out faster.

Several more minutes passed in silence. Katherine flipped over to her messages and started answering one but shut it down after only a few words. She couldn't concentrate. The lump in her throat and her racing heart wouldn't subside.

The panel chimed. Samantha's eyes seemed brighter, more alert. And more intense. She also wore a white bathrobe now. "You have a plan?"

"Partially. It's a working idea at the moment. I thought that we could—"

She raised a silencing hand. "I don't want to know."

"Why not?"

"Let me put it like this. Ethics Laws no longer apply, so long as you don't get caught."

Katherine cocked her head. She struggled to keep her mouth from hanging open. "What?"

"Do whatever you can, however you can. Don't get caught."

Katherine sat still, staring in disbelief at the screen.

"You're on your own. Do not contact me again until it's over."

A chill ran through Katherine's body.

"Connection terminated," chirped the computer.

Confusion suffocated Katherine's rage and grief.

So long as you don't get caught.

The words echoed inside her head, churning and grinding their way into places once off-limits. She could drop biogenetic weapons on Coalition headquarters. She could infect the entire Coalition with a mutagenic virus.

She could bring the Alliance into the war.

Suddenly, drones didn't seem the right course of action. She could do anything, as long as she could live with herself in the morning.

Katherine lifted her chin. She was going to end the war.

So long as you don't get caught.

CHAPTER FIVE

Reports and messages piled up in the digital sense of the phrase. Cargo manifests, crew reassignments, repair updates, intelligence updates, and battle plans in case of a Coalition attack on the docking port. That was on top of the usual bureaucracy that came with commanding a space port. Katherine stared at the bottom corner of her computer screen.

Messages: 174

She pinched the bridge of her nose, unable to press away her mounting frustration. Twenty-eight hours of reflection and a drug-induced sleep should have presented some ideas. Oh, it had presented ideas. Too many of them, in point of fact. Her brain had been on overdrive since her conversation with Admiral Ortora the previous day.

Messages: 186

Katherine sighed and stood up from her desk. She opened up the hand-carved, cherry-stained wooden box on her far wall, the one that passersby couldn't see as they walked by her transparent doors. She took three darts from the side door. Stepping back near her desk—but not so near that anyone could see her playing—she aimed at the red bull's-eye and fired three darts in quick succession at the corkboard.

One missed entirely, embedding itself into the wooden frame. She frowned. It appeared her brain wasn't the only thing frozen. Her limbs weren't much better.

The admiral's words kept echoing in her mind. The Ethics Laws were the highest laws of the Union, a moral compass steering them through a bleak and grey universe. Like many in the fleet, Katherine saw the compass as what caused the war in the first place. The Coalition looked at the Union and saw a bloated, weak empire, too busy with recreating the ancient days of artisans and philosophers than protecting its borders and developing new weaponry. Like any good predator, the Coalition could sense easy prey.

Even in war, however, Fleet admiralty would never turn their collective backs on the Ethics Laws. That's why Sam Ortora's comment shocked Katherine into silence. Though vague, the implied order in her words hung in the background, taunting her to betray her morals.

Do not contact me again until it's over.

She needed perspective before driving herself insane. Katherine turned away from the game and tapped her communications panel. "Francis to Commander Roberts."

"Yes, Captain?"

"Please come into my office."

Her second-in-command entered the office moments later. He glanced at the darts still in her hand and asked, "Slow day?"

She eyed him. Black streaks covered the sleeves of his grey uniform and a hand-width section of his white hair. His clothes were greased with oil spots. "What happened to you? Looks like a shuttle tried to land on you."

John laughed. "Windrunner's console stopped working. All the engineers are working on the conduit issue right now, so I crawled into the engineering shaft to fix it. I forgot how dirty it was down there."

A faint smile formed on her lips. She motioned to a small, round table in the corner. "John, I need your advice on something." He nodded and sat at the table. She joined him after picking up the thermos of coffee from her desk. John turned over two of the mugs on the table and Katherine poured the steaming liquid out.

Katherine took a sip of the bitter beverage and grimaced.

Coffee was only drinkable after eight or nine sugar cubes, and Perdition had run out of sugar three days ago. "It's a hypothetical situation. In a universe without rules, how would you end the war?"

John choked on his coffee. "What?"

Katherine raised her eyebrows.

He placed his mug on the table and leaned forward. "You're serious." He ran a shaky hand through his hair and looked around, nervously. "Is there a hidden camera in here or something?"

Katherine folded her arms, leaning back in her chair. "You're the master of the universe. What would you do?"

"No rules, huh? I'd turn a few thousand folks suffering from massive depression into heroes by strapping biogenetic weapons to their ships and suicide crashing into every Coalition planet."

She rolled her eyes, her shoulders slumping. "Even if Ethics Laws didn't apply, I'd rather surrender than do that." It was one thing to bend to rules. It was another to kill innocent people. She'd be no better than the Coalition. Perhaps even worse. She'd be a hypocrite doing that while wearing the uniform. Besides, she doubted even Sam would approve of that rather gruesome plan. "Let's say in a universe with some rules."

He laughed this time. "We can't defeat the Coalition. Our only hope is to bring the Alliance into the war."

An annoyed grunt escaped her lips. "I've heard that one before."

John threw his hands up. "Bringing the Alliance into the war is the only way. We aren't big enough or strong enough. We'd like to think we are, but everyone knows the Union is bent over the ship's hull. The Alliance has almost double our military force and more advanced weapons technology than anyone. The Coalition wouldn't stand a chance against both of us."

Katherine stared at her coffee mug for a moment. "The Alliance has their Neutrality Agreement with the Coalition. They won't side with us. We're not exactly buddies."

"In the no-rules universe, I'd find a way to see if the Coalition was planning to invade the Alliance after they were done with us. Predators are always looking for their next meal."

Katherine clicked her tongue against the roof of her mouth, pondering. His words made sense, almost too much. She faced a no-rules scenario. While she could not combine suicide bombers and the ability to sleep ever again, she could organize a little espionage to gain a new ally. Not only was it doable, but it wouldn't cost a single life. The plan grew on her, gaining strength from her anger, frustration, and war weariness.

Logic and sense were pushed to the side. It didn't matter that she'd never done anything remotely resembling espionage in her career and had skipped the optional courses at UFU. She could make it work. More importantly, she'd been given the permission.

The door chime rang. Katherine groaned but said, "Come in."

A stout, middle-aged man stepped through the doors, a large data pad in hand. "Good afternoon, Captain. It's lovely to see you. You as well, Commander Roberts. Always a pleasure to see your smiling face." His voice and smile were bright and sunny, annoyingly so.

Roberts sneered but remained silent.

"Good afternoon, Salim." Katherine stood and reached out her hand to accept the pad. She pressed her thumb against it and waited for the verification beep. "Finished already?"

"Indeed. I successfully decoded all the transmissions. Most were quite easy. Coalition security is not what it used to be. Sad, really. They've become sloppy in war. It hurts me to see my people lose their efficiency in wartime. We military zealots need to be efficient at all times, or a turncoat might break one of the communications codes." He smiled, the way he always did when he talked about the Coalition, like there was a private joke that Katherine had not been let in on.

John grunted before saying, "Intel says Coalition security standards have doubled in efficiency since the beginning of the war."

Katherine glanced at John before giving Salim a quizzical look. "Perhaps the security seems lax because they don't know their former spymaster has broken their codes?"

His spine straightened a bit more. "You've been reading mystery novels, haven't you? Spymaster!" He gave her a bashful look and said, "Besides, it is only one code. They have hundreds, if not thousands."

Katherine grinned, even though John maintained his sneer. She stepped over to her computer and added her thumb print for verification. The document uploaded a few seconds later. She handed back the pad. "I'll get these to Intel immediately."

He inclined his head. "Anything to bring an end to this cruel, cruel war."

John cocked an eyebrow. "Anything to get you your own Class 3 communications channel."

Salim flashed a wide, toothy grin that starkly contrasted against his dark skin. "And you say you don't understand me, Commander." He nodded to Katherine before leaving the office.

"What a strange, little man," Roberts said, shaking his head.

Katherine sat down and picked up her coffee again. She sipped and wrinkled her nose. Undrinkable without sugar. "A hell of a decoder, though. Broken one completely and has three others partially deciphered."

"I know he's working for our side. I know he's not a Coalition spy, at least, not anymore since his exile from there. He's broken the Coalition codes, something not even Intel's decoders could do. But, I can't seem to completely trust him."

"Completely? John, I wouldn't trust that man to water my plants. Thing is, Intel trusts him to decode and, you know, so do I. We've known him a long time. As long as we remember that he will do what benefits him the most, we'll be fine."

John looked toward the doors. Windrunner walked by, almost succeeding in looking nonchalant. Almost. "I'm not done repairing Lori's console. We done here? She'll start whining if

I take too long."

Katherine flashed him a smile. "That's all. Thanks for letting me brainstorm."

"Anytime." He stood, taking the coffee mug with him. He stopped before opening the door. "Why did you ask?"

She had never openly lied to John in her life. She took a deep breath and steadied herself. "A friend in Intel wanted to know what folks on the front lines thought. I figured I'd ask, you being opinionated and all."

He seemed placated by the response, though guilt gnawed at her. Lying was never her strong suit. Perhaps that espionage idea wasn't the best plan for her.

After John left the room, she headed over to her desk and collapsed into the padded chair. Three levels of ID verification before the main computer agreed to open Salim's decrypted messages. Her eyes dropped to the lower screen.

Messages: 291

She pulled up the files from Salim on her pad and absently flipped through the translations, decoding, and his footnotes and comments. It contained everything from meaningless fragments of words to fully deciphered messages. She'd forward the fragments and partial messages to Intel's office on Ajax, the planet they orbited with one of their approved officers. The paranoia over the possibility of the Coalition discovering Salim was ripping apart codes had reached such a fevered pitch that no mention of it could be sent over the data Net.

Katherine scanned the full messages, some several sentences long. Most came from the Coalition Star Ship *Sparta.* The *CSS Sparta* was commanded by the tactical genius, Captain Frederick Anderson, and stationed on the other side of sector space. Katherine's job was to skim the messages, catch anything major, and forward the rest to the Intel group on Perdition, who posed as cargo inspectors and, incidentally, were among the best inspectors she'd ever seen.

Her eyes stopped at several lines of numbers. *Sector coordinates.* She transferred them to John's computer and opened a channel. It took a moment before he answered. "Yes, Captain?"

"I sent you sector coordinates. Why do they look familiar?"

"That's the course our next convoy is taking to Outpost Fourteen to resupply them."

"Damn it," Katherine muttered under her breath. "Send an encrypted message to Captain Rayworth immediately. Advise him to change his flight plan. There is a Coalition attack waiting for them."

"Right away." The connection closed.

Katherine leaned back in her chair, using her feet to swivel it back and forth. For whoever Salim was or pretended to be, he saved Union lives every day by decoding transmissions of his own people. Whatever his reason, he also wanted to see the war end. Their motives were the same.

The thought hit her. Salim could help. Salim had a four-hundred-page file and had been under surveillance by Intel for over two decades. And while no one could prove it, Intel would bet its secrets that Salim had indeed been a Coalition assassin, responsible for dozens of high-ranking deaths. Perhaps *the* Coalition assassin.

Who better than a spy to help bring a new ally into a war?

CHAPTER SIX

Staring at Salim across her office desk, Katherine pretended to sip at her coffee. It was too hot to drink, but it kept her from fidgeting. She stared at the top of Salim's thick, black hair and waited. He was hunched over a data pad, elbow on the desk, cradling his chin.

Katherine looked past Salim and watched the traffic of OPs personnel steadily increase outside her glass doors. People slowed as they looked in, curiosity clearly marked on their faces. They'd scurry off when she met their gazes, of course. No doubt OPs buzzed with gossipy questions. No deciphering reports arrived from Intel today, so Salim shouldn't have been needed. Even John and Lori, whose backs were to her office, looked over their shoulders every few minutes.

"Well?" she snapped, impatient for an answer. The fate of the entire Union of Planets rested with him, a man whose Intel file was the size of a planetary survey report. She resigned herself to being desperate and needing his help. She didn't, however, resign herself to spending the entire afternoon with him.

He raised two fingers, signaling that he wasn't finished reading. She absently sipped her coffee and winced when the steaming beverage burned her tongue. Salim glanced up at her and gave her a wry smile. She put her mug down on the table, her cover blown.

Every space port had its own version of a Salim Tobin at one time or another. For all intents and purposes, he was a civilian, running a lucrative toiletries shop near one of the docking ring exits. Apparently, "Salim's Sundries" was *the* shop to hit for front-line soldiers visiting Perdition on an R & R. While Katherine appreciated good soap as much as the next person, she didn't quite understand the near-religious following of his store.

Nevertheless, his shop boosted morale nearly as much as an organics shipment. She had no place to complain, especially since his time deciphering codes was practically charity. He only requested additional cargo storage and a Class 3 Communications link, allowing him triple the priority of his personal messages and double his daily communications allowance. Security monitored his messages periodically, but he seemed to only be doing business deals. She didn't believe it, but she also didn't believe he was betraying them.

Getting Salim involved could become rather sticky, but she needed him.

Salim gasped and followed that with a soft chuckle. He cocked his head and chewed on one side of his mouth. Katherine raised an eyebrow, but he paid no attention to her.

She'd known him for nine years, since her assignment to Perdition. Officially, he had been exiled from Coalition space for tax evasion and loitering in front of government buildings. Considering that there was a standing kill-on-sight order if he re-entered his homeland's borders, Katherine had begrudgingly approached him for assistance helping with basic translations of some Coalition dialects. She didn't trust him, but Command suggested he could assist with building a decoding program.

He had accepted the job offer with childlike glee, saying that his mind was starved of a good challenge. Three days on the job, and Salim broke the news that no one computer program could be designed to decipher the messages. Even if one could be developed, the actual messages would make little sense. He likened it to the Union Fleet using references from Homer, Jane Austen, and current culture to transmit their messages.

So while Intel struggled with short sentences, Salim decoded an entire day's worth of transmissions in under two weeks.

His work had revealed the location of two secret shipyards, allowing the Union to strike one of the most critical blows of the war against the Coalition. With Intel's prodding, she allowed him to decode all manner of intercepted messages in the sector.

Salim placed the pad on the table and folded his hands over it.

A murderous son of a bitch, but she needed him. She licked her lips. "Well? What do you think?" she asked, keeping her voice steady, not wanting him to hear any anxiety.

His eyes narrowed as he looked directly at her. "You want me to enter Alliance space, break into a communications array, and make it appear as though the Coalition did it during one of their 'trade' routes through the system?"

"Well," she said, internally wincing at the slight crack in her voice, "you've twisted it and simplified it, but yes."

Hands still folded, he extended one index finger and pointed at the data pad. In a soft voice, he said, "I thought you liked me, Captain."

She blinked. "Pardon?"

"This is a suicide mission."

Katherine shifted her weight. She knew her plan didn't have much substance to it; she had never drawn up an espionage plan, not even in UFU. Still, she had hoped for a more positive response. "I would have thought, considering your colorful history, that you'd want to use your skills to help bring an end to the conflict. Keep your own people alive."

He leaned back in his chair, raising his hands in the air. "My dear Captain. You have me confused with someone else. My past is merely a boring laundry list of odd jobs and failed business ventures."

Katherine gave him a knowing glare. Though they had rarely spoken about his background, everyone on Perdition had heard the rumours about Salim's history as a spy.

He shrugged his shoulders and tapped the middle finger of his left hand, his index finger being little more than a stump. She never did know why he didn't have a biosynthetic digit graphed to replace the missing finger. "I suppose it wouldn't hurt to make some inquiries amongst my business associates in the toiletries business. Perhaps one of them has had a colorful history as well, as you call it. And, besides, one must keep well informed. A few questions wouldn't do any harm."

"You have connections in the..." She paused, choosing her words carefully. If Salim wanted to play word games, she would, too. "Toiletries business? Can they be trusted? I'd like to keep this as blacked out as possible."

He inclined his head.

Katherine snorted, surprising herself. She looked away for a moment. Tension rose in her. "So you'll help?"

"I'll make a few discreet, casual inquires. It's the least I can do." He rose from the table, leaving the pad. "One more thing, Captain. Is anyone else aware of your plan?"

The overwhelming sensation of being backed into a corner washed over Katherine. She pondered lying, but it wouldn't prove much. Salim wasn't the type to be easily intimidated. "No." She stood to walk him to the door.

He grunted, chewing on his lower lip, deep in thought. "In that case, it might be prudent to remove the security monitoring of my computer access, my communications lines, and my messaging service."

Katherine blinked. Beyond herself, the only other person who knew about those features was Perdition's head of security, Commander Nova Ambrose.

"Dear me. Captain, you look like you're about to faint. Are you all right? You must have stood too quickly. The blood flow from the brain can do that."

She stared at him, unable to form the words. When Salim moved to Perdition, she had three straight days of meetings with Command to review security features, monitoring, and all kinds of training on recognizing undercover operatives.

She swallowed and gained control her voice. "I don't know what you're talking about, Salim. However, I will personally ensure that your deep space communications credits are increased.

Let me know if you have any issues."

Katherine frowned, wondering how to convince Ambrose to stop monitoring Salim's every move.

He bowed. "Thank you. Now, I must be off. There are three ships returning from the front today, and I need to get my store ready for all those weary, tired soldiers in need of a good bath. It is a busy life, if a bit heavy on the floral scents."

Katherine plastered on a fake smile and watched the doors whoosh closed behind Salim. She turned and collapsed into her chair, a sick feeling washing over her. Make no mistake, she needed help and needed help from someone outside of the Fleet. She couldn't shake the feeling that she had asked the devil for a hand up.

CHAPTER SEVEN

Four very long days later, the message came. Salim had news and wanted to meet at his shop. It was a little before seven in the morning. Full brightness lights had not flickered on yet; they wouldn't for another thirty minutes. Perdition's unstable third reactor core had forced Katherine to switch to an eight hour low-lighting period a month ago. Katherine decided that she preferred the artificial night, as she walked through the corridor of the marketplace. It had a planet-side feel to it, even with the metal and glass setting.

The traffic had increased even in the last few moments. The majority of shops were still closed. Most could not afford the extra costs of opening during Perdition's artificial night. Between the challenges of round-the-clock staffing to the high costs Katherine levied on shops wanting to stay at full power during the low-light periods, very few stayed open.

The fourth duty rotation was about to end with the first about to start. A transport ship had docked, two hours ahead of schedule. The ring's double blast doors whooshed open and closed every few minutes, letting another traveller enter Perdition's heart.

She looked around. There was something calming about it all; the passage of time seemed more real here than the digital updates on a clock. It impressed upon her the need for alacrity in bringing the Alliance into the war.

"Good morning, Captain Francis," an ample-hipped

woman said as she pushed an air-assist cart of goods into her tailoring shop. Katherine couldn't remember the woman's name, only that her sister was a sushi chef. Either way, the woman hurried toward her shop, no doubt wanting to open to take advantage of the early arrival of the transport.

Katherine waved back. She also nodded to the cobbler, whose lights flicked on. A pang of sadness hit her when she saw that the sweet confections shop was still dark and not because she wanted one of their hand-made peppermint pops. The shop owner's only daughter had been amongst the confirmed dead when the report came out of Pious III.

Katherine averted her eyes and concentrated on smiling and waving morning greetings to passersby; anything to avoid visiting her own grief. She had not dealt with it nor did she plan to for a long time. It had been conveniently stored away in a neat little compartment in the farthest region of her brain, despite her knowing that the ultimate collapse later would be all the more catastrophic. For now, she had a war to end.

Salim's Sundries was dark, its latticed security gate still locked. She stopped in front of the shop and noticed movement in the shadows inside, announcing Salim's presence. She rapped on the translucent door. The faint aroma of floral perfume tickled the air and her nose.

"I'll be right there," Salim's voice, muffled and distant, called from inside the shop.

As she stood there, Katherine caught herself scanning the area and giving only brisk nods to those who spoke to her in passing. She didn't want to be seen in public with Salim. It was one thing for him to bring reports to her office. It was another to be seen visiting his shop during off-hours. Still, the less she had him in OPs the better. She didn't need John or one of the others asking awkward questions.

A lock clicked. The chain from the security door prevented Salim from fully opening it. As usual, he sported rather bland clothing, a grey sweater with black trousers. Katherine wondered if it was to better blend into his surroundings, or because he didn't like color.

"Ah, good morning, Captain. Just the officer I was hoping to run into today. I say, this is rather fortuitous. One might call it a matter of providence."

"Good morning." Katherine plastered a smile on her face, one that she was sure did not reflect in her eyes. Her muscles tensed. He made no gesture to invite her inside. "Can I come in?"

"Of course!" He began unlatching the security gate so the shop door would swing completely open. "How thoughtless of me. Of course, you'd want to pick up your parcel."

Katherine stared at him and whispered, "Parcel? What parcel? You said you wanted to talk to me."

He finished fumbling with the locks and spoke a bit louder than usual. "And I don't mind opening the shop early for you. After all, our good captain needs to relax and enjoy herself, too, right? No one would fault you for putting in an order of exotic bath oils and pleasure trinkets."

Katherine's eyes widened as her entire body clenched. Heat rose in her cheeks. While she didn't want anyone asking uncomfortable questions about her visiting Salim before hours, she certainly did not want people thinking about her and *pleasure trinkets.*

She glared at him. Hard. Somehow, someway, he would pay for that remark. Katherine pictured him spending a month on sanitation duty as punishment for littering or some other trumped-up charge.

Salim didn't seem to notice her ire, annoying her all the more. "Oh, where are my manners! Here I am, chatting away to arguably the busiest person in the sector. Your order arrived last night on the *Lindsey.* Come on in. I don't open for another hour, but I'll make an exception for our fearless captain."

A long, annoyed sigh screamed to exit her lips, but Katherine held back such unprofessional behavior. Instead, she rolled her eyes when he turned his back to her. As John would say, eye rolling to the face is rude. Eye rolling behind one's back is expected.

Katherine stepped through the opened door into the still dark room and sneezed. Salim flipped on a set of lights. Citric acid dust from bath products floated in the air, casting a dusty haze wherever the light beams hit it. Too many scents mixed together, creating a sickly-sweet perfume. She sneezed again.

Katherine followed him around the various metal stands and display cases of toiletries toward the back of the shop. She sneezed several times. The soap "rose petals" stand was particularly pungent, and three loud, body-shaking sneezes stopped her in her tracks. When she looked up from her sleeve, a white tissue dangled in front of her.

She had never been in his shop before, not being a floral scents person. "How do you work here?" she asked, wiping her nose, aware of the nasal sound of her voice.

He chuckled and said, "I worked sanitation for three years in a labor stockade for violent civilians. After that, very little bothers me."

Katherine twitched at his nonchalant laugh but quickly recovered and kept walking. She'd read about his stint on...she forgot the name of the planet. She did remember, however, that eight prisoners had died under suspicious and unexplained circumstances while he was there.

Salim looked back over his shoulder. "Don't look so surprised, Captain, that Intel got one thing right in my file." He let out a laugh.

Katherine froze. "How do you know about your Intel file?"

He stopped, turning to face her. "Why, Captain, didn't you order security to interrogate me for several hours upon my arrival at the station?"

"No." That was the truth, though she knew it had happened.

He eyed her for a moment and seemed satisfied with her answer, almost as though he could read her thoughts. A chill went through her.

"Well, they did, Captain. No one seems to believe I was

convicted of tax evasion. It's quite humiliating, really."

"Don't forget the loitering charge." She folded her arms, her nose twitching from being so close to a stand of flower-shaped soaps. "The Coalition exiled you from their space and issued a kill order if you stepped inside their borders again."

Salim nodded. "Taxes are very serious back home."

Katherine sneezed and groaned.

"With your sensitive nose, let's go into my office as opposed to staying out here in the storeroom. You might die of dust inhalation, and I'll be accused of murder. How horrific and terrifying that would be." His last sentence was flat and humorless, though his eyes twinkled.

Katherine's heart pounded. She eyed the office door for a moment, watching him enter. The thought crossed her mind that she could be walking into a death trap, and no one would know before it was too late. He'd never get away with it, of course. Her implants were programmed to alert the security system in case her vitals flat-lined; a safety precaution all the senior staff had installed into their hearts after the outbreak of the war. It simply wouldn't make her any less dead.

She was a human test subject for the new medical nanites, who floated dormant in her blood stream, awaiting an emergency. They might keep her alive if Salim...

He gave her an amused, quizzical look, taking years off his middle-aged face. "Captain? I guess I shouldn't have said murder." He chuckled. "If you prefer, we can speak out here."

Katherine looked at him, shaking her head. She had not realized she had been standing there, simply staring at him. "No, of course not. Let's speak in your office."

Salim's spotless office caused Katherine a tinge of envy. Slim, finger-sized data drives were neatly organized in a shallow metal tray with bright labels such as "mystery," "science fiction," "shop orders," and a curiously named, "ways to annoy security." She'd have to ask him about that one later. A small sketch board hung on the wall over his desk with notes about backorders and requests in presumably his own handwriting.

She had one in her office, too. She'd given up using it after losing several styluses. A small air purifier hummed on top of a tall, narrow steel cabinet.

The room was long and narrow, so Salim walked in first and sat at his desk. She sat in the small chair resting against the wall, closer to the door. A rush of claustrophobia swept over her. At least, she noted, she didn't have to sit across from his desk. It would give him authority and she wouldn't have liked that feeling.

Eager to get down to business and back to her job, she asked, "Have you made any progress?"

He crossed his legs and folded his hands over his lap. "I have, Captain."

"And?" Katherine didn't bother to hide the annoyance in her voice.

"I contacted some of my business partners. Many of them are out of favor with the current administration for various reasons far too complicated to explain. Mostly related to additional loitering, littering, and tax evasion. Petty crimes, really. Their...*pursuits* are being hampered by the war, so they have been working to bring an end to the conflict. In discovering we were in fact allies in a common goal, together we developed a bold, uncompromising plan to bring the Coalition to its knees," said Salim, gesturing widely at the last sentence.

She cocked an eyebrow. "Bold and uncompromising?"

Salim shrugged, a slight tinge of blush shaded his dark features. "I have an extensive collection of mystery novels that span the entire genre. I've been reading Sherlock Holmes, and I think the dialogue of his time is taking over."

Katherine resisted a smile. Instead, she tipped her head and said, "You said 'we.' I thought you didn't want to actively help."

His eyes twinkled. "I said that I wouldn't go on a suicide mission, not that I wouldn't offer my assistance. There is a rather large difference between the two. This plan is brilliant. A man who enjoys a good mystery novel like myself could never say no."

Katherine's heart sped up at Salim's excited tone. "That sounds promising."

A frown spread across his face. "Unfortunately, most of them are dead."

Katherine blinked. "Pardon?"

"It appears communications from me are flagged in the Coalition security systems. Something about me being a criminal or some such." He waved a dismissive hand. "I'd admire such swift brutality if it wasn't hampering my ability to do a job."

Her shoulders slumped, guilt washing over her. Working under her name, Salim's communications had caused the deaths of innocent people. She blew out a long breath. She had not expected that. It had not even occurred to her that people would die. A flush of embarrassment over her naivety washed over her.

"Were these friends of yours?"

He shrugged a non-committal gesture. "Think of them as business associates."

She stared at him for a brief moment before saying, "I am sorry that you lost... *business associates* helping me."

And she meant it. Death was a part of command and definitely a part of war. Her plan was to reduce deaths, not increase them. Regardless of who these people were, or their pasts, Katherine had not wanted to bring them harm.

She began to stand. "Thank you for trying. Perhaps the border drones remained the best option after all." She would speak to John and Lori when she got back to OPs.

A pinched looked of disappointment spread across Salim's dark face. "Drones?"

She sat back down. "We could build automated communications drones along the hot spots of the Alliance border. They'd be able to get messages through the jamming signals better than ships." The words were out and she wanted to smack herself. She'd just revealed one of their defensive plans to Salim.

Salim gave her a patronizing smile. "Drones. Interesting."

Katherine shifted uncomfortably in her chair. Well, she'd already let it slip. "What's wrong with that plan?"

He raised his hands. “Absolutely nothing. I think you should do it. I’ve never understood this obsession with not appearing aggressive to your neighbors. Right now, the Union is little more than a ship in systems failure. The scavengers are circling.” He leaned forward. “But, you need more than drones.”

She stood straighter. “I know. We need the Alliance on our side.”

He nodded, remaining silent.

“But how? The only way was to—” She stopped, her mouth gaping open. She flicked her eyes to the “mystery” data drive, no doubt filled with thousands of novels. It gave her an idea; an insane, illegal, plan. “We can create the necessary documents. Frame the Coalition for something. Withholding tech, selling state secrets, that sort of thing.”

Salim smiled while her stomach rolled. What she was suggesting was wrong. It was beyond wrong. It was impossible. She felt ill even saying the words, and yet they felt right. In the no-rules universe scenario, this was an option. Of course, she could never live with herself.

She waved off her own words. “That’s a fantasy plan. Ignore me. It’s comparable to Commander Roberts’s plan of strapping biogenetic weapons to a bunch of soldiers with torpedo shock.” She leaned back in the chair, shoulder slumping. “What was the bold plan you and your friends came up with?”

Salim chewed his lower lip and shook his head. “You really won’t like it.”

“I don’t like sending teenagers to die, but I do it.” She took a sharp breath. “What is the plan?”

“It appears we are all on the same page.” He lifted his eyebrows, a mischievous smile across his face. “Concoct whatever evidence you require to bring the Alliance into the war.”

CHAPTER EIGHT

She released a short bark of laughter. “I wasn’t being serious.”

Katherine’s conscience screamed to run from Salim’s backroom office as fast as her legs could carry her. A part of her, the part that had worn the grey Union Fleet uniform proudly for nearly two decades shouted that even entertaining the notion of forgery was treason. Treason not only against the Ethics Laws, either, but against all manner of conscience.

Yet, she had offered and entertained the idea, albeit briefly. To ease her conscience, she reminded herself she had dismissed the idea as soon as she spoke it. Salim, however, already believed it was the perfect plan and defended that belief.

“Excluding the fact that you brought up the idea first,” he scoffed, flicking his hands in the air, “this is no worse than your original plan of breaking into Coalition security systems and blaming it on the Alliance.”

“That was different,” she snapped. Her conscience told her to end the conversation before his twisted logic began to corrupt her. It preached about good intentions and roads and hell. Breaking galactic law, Ethics Laws, and violating her own personal code of honor were all paths to hell. Saving her people from a long, drawn out war was a good intention, but this twisted logic would bring about personal destruction.

“How so, Captain? How is your plan better? Was it because it didn’t dirty your hands?”

Her breath hitched in her throat, his words stunning her into silence. The thought had not crossed her mind before, but Salim was right. The only difference in plans was that her hands would be soiled by this direct route. Her plan would have arranged for Salim's contacts to take the risks while she sat in her office, sipping coffee. How cowardly of her to expect others to do her dirty work; others who ended up paying for her squeamishness with their lives.

Her mind screamed to walk away. Common sense suggested that Salim might not have even contacted anyone, and this was all a part of some twisted scheme. Lying for political gain was against the Ethics Laws, and admiral's approval or not, it was wrong, wrong, wrong.

"Well, Captain?"

Katherine opened her mouth to say no. An image of her baby sister, laughing, flashed into her mind, quelling Katherine's conscience. She let out a sigh. "All right, Salim. I'll listen to your plan."

Her soul felt dirty for even entertaining the thought. Listening did not equate to acceptance, she reminded herself. She reassured herself she would leave if she didn't like what he had to say.

He inclined his head, a small smile wrinkling the corners of his eyes. "As you are well aware, I am a man of many talents. It's from reading mystery novels from the twentieth century. I also do a full mystery holo-vid every month to help keep my mind fresh. I've picked up a few skills along the way."

"Get to the point," she snarled.

A wide, toothy grin spread across his face. "I assume you scanned the shop for surveillance devices."

"Yes." She did it from OPs before setting off to their meeting. A touch of pride filled her. She might be naive about matters of subterfuge, but she was not an idiot. "Though, I was surprised that the internal security features in your shop were not functioning correctly. It's a good thing I caught it. I'll have Security correct the problem."

His dark eyes twinkled approvingly. He looked over his shoulder at the ceiling. He waved and flashed it a big grin. "Captain, there is no end to the pain I feel knowing that Security continues to plant subterfuge devices in here. I understand many personal freedoms need to be curtailed during wartime. But is this really necessary?" He pointed up.

Katherine stood and leaned toward the corner in question. Not far from two meters in height, she was able to get a good look at the low hanging ceiling. A speck of grey dust caught her attention, mostly because dust didn't come perfectly round.

"I scanned the entire shop before I came down here. I have no idea where it came from." Sickness washed over her. She had run every possible surveillance detection program the Union had. If someone had recorded her meeting, even someone within the Fleet, she could lose her commission. If news got out, the Alliance might join the Coalition against them. She stared at Salim and wondered if this would be his first betrayal.

Salim's white teeth glowed as his mouth spread into a wide grin. "Don't worry, Captain. It's a pet project of mine. I'm attempting to make a virtually undetectable surveillance device to catch shoplifters. Right now, it only catches partial video and sound. Not very useful yet."

She cocked her head at him, heat rising in her cheeks. "You have been recording this conversation?"

He raised his hands defensively. "I didn't turn the recording aspect of the device on. I haven't figured out all the wiring to make it work with a neural interface."

"Then why the show?" she asked, near growling in anger.

"OPs has far superior scanning capabilities than I possess. I wanted to make sure you knew to scan every single room before I opened my mouth and landed myself in a Union prison for conspiracy." He folded his arms and grinned. "I've read many a spy novel, Captain. I know how these things work."

She clenched one hand on the edge of her chair. "Do not toy with me. I am here to end a war, not play games."

Gone were his playful features. His eyes turned cold,

hard. "I apologize if I upset you, but my plan will offend your sensibilities. If you cannot handle a little jabbing over security features, you will not only fail in your endeavor, but you will most likely get me killed. And, since my knowledge is merely based on mystery and spy novels," he said, pausing to lean forward, "I'm looking to you to be the professional."

Katherine fumed. "Meaning, you will bring me down before you get caught yourself."

He sat up straight again. His easy smile, the trademark of his features, spread across his face once more. His tone lightened. "I'll be extradited back home where a general execution order awaits me. You'd go to New Zealand's penal colony and talk about your feelings. You see the problem."

"I understand. Now, I want to hear your brilliant plan before my patience and manners leave town."

"Ah yes. The plan. Of course. I will endeavor to stay on topic for your sake. An Alliance delegation is meeting the Coalition in twelve days to negotiate an extension of their non-aggression treaty."

"How do you know that?" Katherine tried not to sound surprised, but his smug smile let her know he had read her body language. "That's classified information."

"A man of my career has many hobbies. Galactic politics is mine."

"Personally, I enjoy growing coffee in the hydroponic gardens. So there will be a meeting. How will that help us?"

Salim stretched out his short legs. "As it happens, one of the lesser Alliance delegates owes me a favor." She raised her eyebrows. "Truly?"

"Arthur Frum." He nodded, grinning. "His little sister once became entangled with the most unfortunate crowd. I helped...extract her."

"All right. We have a lesser delegate. So what?"

"We invite this delegate to meet you in a neutral area." Salim's eyes glittered with excitement, the way a cat brightens when handed a bag of catnip. "You will show him documentation from Coalition military security in which the planned assassination of their senior council is being discussed."

Katherine snorted. "The only war that will come out of your plan is the Alliance attacking us."

Salim shook a displeased finger in the air. "You have so little faith in my abilities. I know I can do it. The question is do you want to trust me?"

She looked away and stared at the surveillance device on his ceiling, her mind balancing the risks and rewards. She knew Salim had been a spy for longer than she had been in the Fleet. He had been a positive and helpful member of the Perdition community since his arrival. Intel had felt comfortable enough to let him work on decoding communications, which meant they did not pick up any reason to distrust him.

But his plan. She would be using someone who owed Salim a favor for rescuing a family member in distress. Being a captain in the Fleet meant she protected, not took advantage of people. She would be violating the entire reason she wore the uniform.

Still, his plan had merit. Katherine hesitated. "I should clear this with Command."

He shook his head. "You said they wanted to know as little as possible, which I believe means they gave you *carte blanche*."

That surprised her. "You speak French?"

"Of course. All civilized humans do."

She sighed. When she answered him, she chose her words carefully, fearful of giving him too much information about her conversation with Sam. "They gave me leniency to investigate how to end the war, not to break galactic law."

"My dear Captain. You truly understand nothing about subterfuge. Don't they teach basic espionage in captain school? If you ask your superiors for permission, they will deny your request. They would have to. But if you, by your own quiet means, bring the Alliance into the war on our side, they won't care how you did it."

Her heart and mind waged a war against each other. There was a difference between bending some rules, turning a blind eye to certain shady deals. Throwing her ethics out the door was another thing altogether.

"I need to think about this."

She stood, Salim following her example a second later. As she turned to leave his office, he said, "I suggest that you think quickly."

She didn't answer, or even turn to face him. Instead, she walked out of his office, past the smelly soaps, sneezed twice, and headed back into the corridors. Her heart sagged.

She couldn't do it.

She wouldn't do it.

There had to be another way.

CHAPTER NINE

Katherine sat in the weekly meeting, absently staring at Raewadee as she went through the items engineering needed. Considering the amount of traffic they handled, Perdition's needs list was extensive.

Katherine only absorbed bits and pieces. Something about a lack of sealants and capacitors holding up the bulk of the repairs. Perdition needed another industrial fabricator. Her focus remained fixed on her talk with Salim earlier that morning.

She faded into her checklist, a list of reasons why she should reject his plan. First, it was wrong. It seemed trite, but she felt it important to mentally verbalize it all the same. In amongst all the justifications and convoluted logic, Katherine reminded herself she hesitated because, deep down, she knew Salim's plan was ethically wrong. So why couldn't she shake the feeling that no better plan existed?

"I sent fifteen of the least damaged ships to Ajax's civilian shipyard. They are willing to help with basic repairs, and Admiral Ortora gave the Engineering Corps clearance to outsource..."

Katherine's attention strayed at the Admiral's name. Sam had given her a wide berth, with her cryptic, "so long as you don't get caught" speech. Katherine couldn't deny that she still liked her automated communication drone plan. True, it pushed the Ethics Laws and might open up debate, but it was still on the right side of right. Salim's plan was so radical, so disgusting, that she couldn't go ahead with it. Surely, it wasn't what Sam had meant.

As she watched her senior officers, all taking notes and asking questions that she barely heard, the core question of the matter pounded at her, demanding an answer. Why was Salim's plan so disgusting to her?

She struggled to find an answer that didn't resemble a Fleet handbook to recruits. No, she would honor her uniform and use the drones to bring about a dignified end to the war. Surprise attacks were partially how the Coalition was still winning. Reducing their opportunities would increase the Union's chances of survival.

Katherine pushed aside the faces of her loved ones, no doubt dead or wounded on Pious III. They would not want her to sacrifice her ethics for them.

Someone coughed. "Captain?"

Katherine snapped her head up and stared at Raewadee. She swallowed her embarrassment for fading out and said, "Yes, thank you Lieutenant. Please make your report accessible to all senior officers and department heads."

The dark-skinned woman nodded and sat down. All eyes fell on Katherine. She cleared her throat. "I suppose it's my turn." A weary laugh escaped her. She stood up and stepped to the front of the table. "The last time we were here, it was too warm. Now, it's too cold. One day, this meeting room will be at optimum temperature again."

She forced a small smile at the five officers in front of her. Katherine looked at her data pad; the updates had finally stopped downloading. "I'll post the details of everything later today, but I'll run through the basics."

She fiddled with the red pad. "Seven ships reported destroyed in the last twelve hours."

Roberts raised his hand to catch her attention. "Why so few?"

"Ah," she mumbled as she flipped through the files. She had never been this unprepared for a meeting in her life. "Intel believes the Coalition is gearing up for another offensive. The details are pretty sketchy, but..." She trailed off and shrugged.

She took a deep breath to center herself. "I'm sorry, everyone. I'm not prepared. I'd like to skip the usual laundry list and suggest something. Command asked all Fleet captains, myself included, to come up with ideas to end the war faster. I've been given the go ahead for an automated drone system." A mild lie, but she couldn't tell them she was given leeway to step on the Ethics Laws. They might assume it, but assumptions were very different than confirmation.

Her staff remained still, as if they held their breath. No one even fidgeted. She felt encouraged by their lack of questions. They wanted more information.

"The Coalition is able to invade our space because they use Alliance territory, which borders our own in several places. They have the ability to jam ship communications so posting ship sentries has failed miserably. But drones run on a number of different frequencies."

That caught Lieutenant Commander Williams' attention, and he perked up. "Even if the Coalition jams one frequency, the drones could bombard all the others with a warning signal."

"And, we could put a small cluster of messenger drones with them. So, if one goes dead, the others will take off in different directions, broadcasting the signal," Raewadee said, a broad smile forming. "With so many different drones broadcasting on Union frequencies, something will get through."

Williams blurted, "Coalition ships would eventually adapt but not for a while. In the meantime, these drones will make it significantly difficult to sneak into our territory without us knowing about it. I love the idea, Captain."

Katherine nodded. "I don't have any particulars or even a draft plan. I don't even know if it's doable yet."

Roberts interrupted her. "With your permission, I'll organize department heads in mechanics, engineering, and communications to brainstorm their ideas."

Her heart sped up, and excitement flushed her. She had come up with a way to slow the Coalition attacks. She did not need to lie, cheat, or violate any laws. Accomplished pride filled her, seeing the eager hope on the faces of her crew.

Excited chatter overtook the room, and Katherine didn't hear the comm signal. She did, however, see the flashing red light on the panel that jutted out of the middle of the conference table.

Katherine tapped it. "Francis here."

"Captain," said Ensign O'Connor. She left him in charge of OPs during the meeting, thinking he could use the experience. "I-I need all of you in OPs. Now!"

Katherine and John jumped to their feet and were out the door before the others' chairs even squeaked. She rushed across the hallway and slapped a hand on the door scanner. Her heart pounded in her throat. Was there an attack? The emergency klaxons weren't signaling, but with OPs full of ensigns and newly-promoted lieutenants, no one might have thought of that.

Katherine stormed into OPs through the second level entrance and rushed toward the stairs to where her own war panel was located on the first floor. She froze. Every communications accessible panel in OPs displayed a visual of the Coalition's War Admiral Sullivan, outdoors, on a cloudy morning.

Sullivan spoke, his voice husky like he smoked too much. "...started this war out of necessity, not out of malice."

Katherine squinted. Something about the area he transmitted from seemed familiar.

"We wanted peace with the Union of Planets. We asked them to join us in an Agreement of Neutrality. They refused."

"Where is this coming from?" Katherine shouted over the volume, still staring at the largest screen directly ahead of her, the one that normally displayed Fleet movements in the sector.

"Don't know, Captain. It's bombarding on all frequencies in the sector." Lieutenant Anders said and frantically tapped at his console. "All I know is that I can't stop it."

Williams resumed his place at the head of Tactical. Windrunner took her place at Communications.

"Working on it now, Captain," Windrunner said, not

looking up, and her fingers flying over both the vertical and horizontal display monitors.

Katherine's three cups of mid-day coffee churned in her stomach. She recognized the mountain formations. Pious III. *Home.*

Using the metal railing for balance, Katherine sprinted down the stairs, sometimes three at a time. She rushed to her console. When O'Connor saw her, he hurried over. Katherine feared he'd faint; he looked so pale and shocked.

"Captain! I didn't know what to do when I couldn't stop the transmission—"

She held up a hand. "You did good. I'm going to put a commendation in your records."

"...attempt to expand our sphere of influence, which can only be expected of a great power such as the Coalition. At no point did we violate undisputed sectors, nor did we threaten violence against those planets under the protection of the Union of Planets. And how was our kindness repaid? With an attack."

Katherine licked her lips, fury rising inside her, as she listened to the passionate man on the screen in his dark green uniform twist the truth into a lie. They had never attacked the Coalition. An exploration convoy into uncharted space was attacked by a Coalition squad on a 'training exercise.' The convoy defended itself. However, war had been declared that day.

"There is no longer a time or a place for peace. We will not sit idly by while the warmongering Union attacks us and attempts to invade planets that are under our protection. We will not allow their violence and intolerance to spread.

"We call for the total surrender of the Union of Planets. Consider that innocent people of the Union die by the millions because their leaders are too short-sighted to realize they have no chance against us. We will defend our interests."

"Come on, people. Let's get this transmission cut," Roberts shouted out over the transmission. Though he shouted, he did not sound annoyed.

"I can't Commander!" O'Connor shouted back, his voice

high-pitched.

Windrunner's voice was calm, the voice of experience." Captain, somehow they've tapped into Pious III's communications array. We can't stop the signal."

"Cut power to the communications here, then," Katherine ordered.

"Can't. They've somehow changed the security override codes. I can't block them."

Katherine frowned. She made a mental note to have a full systems reboot and new encryption protocols drawn up when this was over. "Keep at it. If you have to, sever our incoming link. Engineering will be upset, but it's better than this."

"As proof, enjoy the deaths of your loved ones from Pious III."

A short growl escaped Katherine's lips, but she sucked it back under control. Her family was already dead. "All right, folks, let's cut this transmission. It'll probably be on repeat..."

Katherine stopped speaking, and all chattering in OPs ceased. A grainy, shaky image appeared on the screen. A teenage boy, blindfolded, with his hands tied behind him.

"What's happening?" the boy asked between hiccupping sobs.

Six Coalition soldiers, three men and three women, stood in front of him. The camera operator moved to capture a side angle of the soldiers raising their weapons.

Katherine grabbed the railing next to her, unable to stop herself from shaking.

Blue pulse beams blasted the boy at point blank range, charring his skin. He collapsed to the ground, silent. Smoke twisted in the breeze around him.

"Merciful God," Roberts whispered next to her. She hadn't even known he was there. He crossed himself.

A blindfolded woman was thrown on top of the smoldering corpse. She cried out for help. Weapons rose.

"Cut the feed! Cut it!" Roberts shouted over the dying woman's screams.

"I can't, Commander!" Windrunner shouted.

O'Connor spoke up, his voice quavering. "It's transmitting all through Perdition, Captain. I can't stop it."

Three other junior officers shouted that they couldn't either.

"Cut main power," Katherine bellowed out. "Shut down that transmission."

Weapons blasted. The woman crumbled. Behind Katherine, O'Connor vomited on his console, the acrid stench filling OPs.

Katherine broke into a run before the thought even formed in her mind. She grabbed a long wrench from the floor, next to a dismantled console, and jumped down into the pit, where engineers had been working moments before. Lights and klaxons flashed. Using the wrench, she smashed the electrical panels with all her fury.

A jolt of energy zapped through her. She smelled the faint stench of burning wires.

The sobs of a child filled the air before the world faded into blackness.

CHAPTER TEN

Katherine woke up gasping for air. Ground skimmers were shooting at her. She had to—

Wait. Metal ceiling with exposed piping. Soft, muted light. Strands of piano music playing behind her. Sterile air.

She blinked, her eyes filled with grit. Where the hell was she? What happened to those Coalition ships?

Another focusing blink revealed an iridescent medical field around her body. Her heart pounded. She couldn't remember how she ended up... In the hospital?

Her natural reaction was to push herself up and investigate her surroundings, but she couldn't control anything below her chin. She felt her limbs, her torso, but they refused to obey her. The numbness prevented her from moving, and fear gripped her. Katherine tried to push aside the thought of life in a wheelchair, assisted by robots and friends. The dread threatened to suffocate her.

"Hello?" With her lips and throat parched, the word came out as a hoarse cough. "Hello?"

Katherine struggled to keep her eyes open. The room faded in and out, but with each blink, she grew more alert and aware of her surroundings. Machines hummed and beeped. She heard feet shuffle further away and muted voices. She realized she was alone.

"Hello?" Her words, still hitching in her dry throat, came stronger this time. "Is anyone there?"

"Captain!" Metal clanged against metal. "She's awake. Call Commander Windrunner."

Katherine wondered why the man requested Lori. She exhaled forcefully and counted the approaching footsteps. Hospital. The antiseptic scent should have given it away. A powder blue curtain wisped to one side. Two more footsteps.

A man with a pale, bald head and grey beard leaned over her. Doctor Henry Kramer. She relaxed a little, seeing a familiar face. She was not alone. "Welcome back, Captain."

She struggled to keep her eyes open; the grainy texture of sleep caused her to squint. "I was gone?"

He nodded while inserting a needle into a small glass jar. "For a bit. You gave all of us quite a scare. How are you feeling?"

"I can't move," she said to the middle-aged doctor, fear forcing her to whisper; otherwise she'd break into tears of shock.

"This will fix you right up," he said, motioning to the needle. He tapped the vial before pushing it into her skin. It nipped before a cold, stinging sensation snaked its way inside her arm. "I gave you an inhibitor while you were out to prevent you from hurting yourself when you first woke. I should warn you, though. You will be in a fair bit of...discomfort until you determine the level of pain management you want me to administer."

An agonizing ache developed moments after the injection, her joints screaming louder with each passing second. Blinding agony shook Katherine's threshold. She gasped for air; even breathing was beyond possible.

She regained enough control over her neck to turn toward Henry, who stood to the side of her bed reading her data chart. Katherine's grasp on consciousness slipped. Fearful of blacking out again, she whispered, "Something...it hurts."

Silently, Henry tapped a console attached to her bed, near the medical dome that covered most of her body. Light sparkled across her vision before returning to normal. The screaming pain settled to a dull, pervasive, crippling ache. "That should take the edge off for now. We'll discuss proper pain management after you've seen Commander Windrunner."

"Thank you," she gasped, wondering why he didn't give her something a lot stronger. She would have asked, but her mind still felt like jelly. Speaking remained difficult.

Henry sat on a chair and wheeled himself to her bedside, using his feet. "Do you remember what happened?"

Images flashed in her mind, but she couldn't decipher which were real. She shook her head, wincing. "I remember lights."

"I wager you do," he said, not smiling. "Do you remember the Coalition stream?"

"No. Wait, yes," she said, the doctor's words jolting her memories loose. "I remember O'Connor couldn't cut the feed. There was an explosion."

The doctor nodded as he fumbled to grab the stylus that swung on a string from his pad. "You don't remember anything else?"

"No." She failed to shake her head, though she tried. "How long was I out? And what happened?"

"Nine days." He stopped writing to look at her.

Nine days. Katherine's muscles clenched at that. Endless streams of duties and obligations piled in her mind. "What happened?"

"You jumped into the engineering pit on OPs and smashed a wrench into a communications panel. It sent out a nasty feedback wave that threw you about fifteen meters in the air before you landed on Ensign O'Connor's console. Nearly sent the kid into shock. And, as for you, if it hadn't been for your medical nanites, well, you are a prime example of why everyone in the Fleet should have them." He took a deep breath, tapping his pad more. "Commander Windrunner will fill you in on the specifics of Perdition's situation, I'm sure. She's on her way."

The details explained the body-wide throbbing pain, at least. The doctor reached over her and pressed a button on the wall. It beeped several times.

"Henry, I'd like Commander Roberts to come, too."

The doctor froze for a split second before continuing his note-writing. He swallowed hard, and Katherine noticed shiny beads of sweat pool on his forehead. "Your scans are all negative, which means the nanites have done all that they can. I'd prefer it if you stayed here for a few days for us to manage the pain and begin your rehabilitation, but I doubt you'll agree to that once Windrunner talks with you. I've forwarded your rehabilitation schedule to OPs. If you don't follow it to the letter, I will cite you as medically unable to perform your duties. Have I made myself clear?"

Katherine raised an eyebrow at Henry's threat but inclined her head as best as she could. Henry didn't smile and refused to meet her gaze. Something about the situation seemed off. Frustration mounted as she struggled to use her still-muddled brain. The pieces didn't fit properly, and the neutralizer moved too slowly. She needed to move and to think. "Why isn't Commander Roberts coming?"

"He won't be able to see you right now, Captain. I need you to understand the extent of your injuries. Three cracked ribs, two broken vertebrae, ruptured spleen, various chipped bones, a concussion, internal bleeding, and enough electricity went through your body to power a small shuttle craft."

"Shouldn't I be dead then?" she whispered.

"Three years ago, you would not have made it. The electric current was absorbed by the emergency nanites you've been testing for us. That's why you're still breathing. We then injected you with surgical nanites. They kept you in the coma until you were healed enough to wake up. You will need to split your duties with your entire senior team for at least a month. Maybe two."

A part of her knew she should care about what he said, but the fog of medication and a nine-day coma clouded everything. "I can't believe I was out for over a week." A warm sensation spread through her right hand. Her extremities tingled as feeling slowly returned. She flicked her eyes at him, blinking and trying to focus. "I can't believe I'm alive."

"Even with the nanite repairs and the microsurgery, you'll still need physical therapy. It'll be months before you are pain free. Medication will only help so much."

More fog cleared as the neutralizer left a warm, heated-blanket feeling along her hip. She moved her torso. She took a sharp breath, pushing against the pain. "Did we cut the Coalition transmission at least?"

"Yes." He looked down at the floor. "I have other patients to look after. Commander Windrunner is on her way. She'll explain everything."

Katherine regained enough control over her body to turn her neck and watch the doctor shuffle away. She wondered why Henry was so on edge. Her stomach filled with nervous twitches.

Nine days. What could have happened? The voice of experience whispered many things, none of them particularly good.

Katherine resumed staring at the metal ceiling. The ward with proper walls was for long-term patients. A sense of relief filled her. Being in the temporary ward meant she wasn't injured enough to need long-term care. She'd need rehab, though. Months of recovering while alone. Sure, she had John and Lori, but they were still her staff. Her family was gone. She lived alone these days.

She was alone.

She drew a sharp breath and forced down the grief and hurt. The time would come to grieve; it had not arrived yet. Lori would arrive soon and provide her the rundown of events. After that, she would contact Command, figure out what the hell was going on, and then she would start on her drone plan.

Emptiness filled the spot where the excitement over the drones once lived. The plan lacked the thrill of success now. The Coalition's actions showed the true meaning of boldness in the face of the enemy. They wanted to strike fear into the Union's hearts. A few drones along a border could not compete.

Even Salim's scheme of planting "evidence" was now less extreme in the light of day. The Coalition had changed the game.

"The captain?" Lori asked somewhere in the distance, her

voice muffled. "Thanks." A few steps, and she poked her head through the curtains and into the tiny recovery room. Behind her filed in Raewadee, sporting her dress uniform, and Sister Mary Nora, one of the Fleet clergy assigned to Perdition. Katherine gulped. She was Catholic. That meant Sister Mary Nora was called to deliver the kind of news that one would want coming from a religious person. Her heart raced. "Tell me."

Dark, swollen circles hung under Lori's eyes, and for a moment, Katherine thought the woman had been in a fight. She looked closer. Her knuckles were covered in scabs. She *had* been in a fight. What the hell happened?

"It's good to see you awake, Katherine."

Katherine eased herself up, joints cracking. She grimaced against the steady, pervasive ache that encompassed her entire body. "You look like hell, Lori."

"A lot has happened, Captain," Sister Mary Nora said, her tone muted.

Katherine forced herself up the entire way, pushing aside the demands of her screaming muscles. She did not want to be lying down when the news came. Tears welled in her eyes from the piercing pain, but she pushed through it. "What happened after the Coalition feed?"

Lori licked her lips. "You managed to shut down main power to communications for over two hours. Ships and independent systems still got the feed, however. It took Command five hours to jam the signal in this sector."

Raewadee took a step forward when Lori's voice cracked. "One of the freighter captains saw his wife and children shot on the vid stream. He knew Salim was from the Coalition, and he went to the shop to kill him. It started a riot." She swallowed hard, her voice shaking. "Nineteen people were killed before we could control the situation."

Katherine tilted her head, taking a slow, steady breath. Her heart pounded and echoed in her ears. "Commander Roberts?"

Lori lowered her gaze for a moment before nodding. "I'm sorry, Captain."

"John," she whispered. Then, Katherine's voice turned cold and hard, a storm of anger and grief screamed to be let loose. "How?"

Raewadee answered. "Commander Roberts threw himself on top of Salim to protect him. He was killed by a pulse charge."

"Doc says he went fast," Lori added.

Katherine clenched her jaw until her head felt it would explode from the pressure. "Salim?"

"He's alive. We locked him in containment for a couple of days until we re-established order. The market reopened yesterday. Salim insisted on going back to work, so Ambrose put security all through the market level. She said they're staying until you give the order to remove them."

"Good thinking," she whispered. A small voice in the back of her mind whispered the details of Salim's plan to bring the Alliance into the war. John would understand. John would support it.

Sister Mary Nora cleared her throat and said, "We held the memorials last week. We didn't know when you'd wake, and we couldn't wait any longer."

"I understand." A large lump formed in Katherine's throat, as if she had swallowed a steel ball. She had known John for two decades. They served together three separate times. He'd been the best man at her wedding. His mother sent her a handmade birthday gift every year. She had lost her family and now her best friend. Rage shook her.

Sister Mary Nora caressed her prayer beads, her matronly face filled with quiet compassion. "There's more. There is no easy way to tell you this, Captain. Whatever family you had left on Pious III was..."

Katherine's body tensed when the nun's voice trailed off.

The sister took a deep breath. "Their executions were transmitted. Father LeBlanc and I have made a detailed list of names for you, when you are ready. They executed your entire extended family very cruelly, once the connection with you was made. Then, they destroyed the planet's atmosphere.

I am sorry."

Katherine's jaw quivered. She held back the tears that stung her eyes.

"I called Patricia," Lori said, uncertainty in her voice.

"What?" Anger swelled inside Katherine. "You did what!"

"Katherine." The sister held up her hand and pitched her voice in that stern way only a nun could have. "Be angry with me. I told her to do it."

"How dare you call her?" Katherine clenched her fists until white stars flashed across her vision.

"You were in a coma. Even if you aren't on speaking terms right now, she is your *wife*." Lori snapped, though she drawled out the last word.

Silence hung between them. Katherine looked away from them, allowing the anger to sink and seethe. She wasn't angry at them; calling family members in medical emergencies was policy, not to mention common human decency. She did not want Patricia to see her like this: grieving, angry, and contemplating breaking the law.

When Katherine dared to ask the question, a nervous chill made the hairs on her arm stand on end. "Is she coming?"

Raewadee smiled, one that touched her eyes and brightened them. "By the time we found her in the field, she was already en route. Apparently, she left as soon as the news about Pious III hit her hospital. It's going to take a few weeks. She's on a stealth convoy, so..." Raewadee shrugged. "We don't know exactly when she'll arrive."

"Thank you, *Bindu*," Katherine said, exhaling. She could be on a first named basis with someone who brought her that kind of good news in a sea of grief.

The young woman straightened her shoulders.

Sister Mary Nora smiled. "She's coming, Katherine. We didn't even have to ask her."

A small, fragile smile spread across her face. Patricia was on her way home. Patricia was coming to look after her. For that brief moment, Katherine closed her eyes and let the words comfort and soothe both the physical pain and the grief inside her. It would be nice to have her wife back, even if she didn't stay.

Her mind's voice whispered that Salim's plan could be executed by the time Patricia arrived.

The drones weren't that exciting anymore. The Coalition had crossed the line. So could she. She looked down and noticed she was dressed in fresh, clean clothes. Not her uniform, but not a bathrobe, either. Henry must've known she'd want to work as soon as she woke.

Lori cleared her throat and said, "Lieutenant Raewadee and I have drawn up a schedule. Doc says you need light duties."

Katherine glared at her new Second in Command. "I need a portable comm unit."

This time, Lori's smile was a touch brighter. She pulled a palm-sized, black device from her pocket. A portable communications pad.

"Thanks," Katherine said, taking it. "Let's go. I have work to do."

Katherine pushed herself off the bed. White-hot, blinding pain shot through her. A whimper escaped her. If it hadn't been for her three visitors grabbing her, she would have fallen face-first.

"You stubborn woman," Henry said, as he walked back into the room. "I told you that we'd discuss drugging you out of your senses after Commander Windrunnner was done speaking with you. I never said a thing about discharging you."

Grasping the bed's footboard for support, she forced out, "Take the edge off."

A loud, frustrated sigh escaped him. "The only way to get you pain-free is to dope you. Weren't you listening before? I don't even know how you're standing."

"Pure stubbornness, Doctor," Bindu said, her chin held high. "It's why we'd follow her into the pits of hell."

The rush of pride washing through Katherine almost made the hurt bearable for a moment. Almost.

"Give me enough...to work a couple of hours." Katherine's

hands shook. She didn't know how much longer she could hold on. "Promise to go directly to my quarters after." She drew a breath and struggled against unconsciousness. "Give me the goddamn shot."

He glared at her. She met his gaze and did not look away. Her breathing increased. Her vision blurred. "Drugs. *Now*."

White dots splashed across her vision. Henry broke the stare first. He took a pre-filled needle from a wall dispenser and pressed it into her neck. "It's an endorphin-nanite pain suppressor. You're still going to hurt a lot, but at least your spirits will be high. It'll start working in thirty seconds, but it'll take twenty minutes to reach its full strength. It only lasts for four hours. I'll have a nurse come see you in your room and work out your therapy sessions."

She ignored him and turned to the older woman. "Sister, would you be so kind as to lend me a supportive push? I will need a wheelchair."

"Of course." The nun put her arm around Katherine and helped her into the chair next to the bed. A warm, soothing, *happy* sensation began floating over her. "Let's step outside."

The doctor kept talking, but she ignored him. She had a duty to the people of Perdition, and she would not shirk that responsibility. As they left the facility, she expected to suffer from grief over John, but she didn't. She had rage. Blinding, uncontrollable rage. The kind that sent a cold stream through her blood and covered her skin in prickles.

Sister Mary Nora wheeled her outside. About seventy people were gathered there, no doubt waiting for news after they had seen Lori enter the hospital. They broke into applause, and it nearly broke her. The nun squeezed Katherine's shoulder. Only a member of the cloth would dare touch her while on duty. It didn't bother her, coming from the old nun. Supportive touching was something nuns did.

She lifted a hand to silence them before tapping her comm unit on. After getting the setting to "port-wide broadcast mode," she cleared her throat and spoke into the device. "This is Captain

Katherine Francis of Perdition Docking Port."

She paused to adjust herself to hearing her voice delayed a split second through every single open communications panel throughout the port. "First, I would like to thank everyone who assisted with saving my life. I am well enough to resume duties as captain, though I will be sharing them with Commander Windrunner for a few weeks upon the advice of the medical team."

Another pause. Her body ached, but she pushed it aside. She had a duty to these people to restore their hope and faith. "I have been brought up to speed on what has happened in the last nine days. I am sorry I was unable to be there to protect the lives that were lost. Let their deaths not be in vain. Let's never forget that it was the Coalition that killed our families and our friends. They are who we are supposed to fight, never each other."

Her voice gained strength as the anger bubbled up to the surface. She didn't stop it. Instead, she allowed it fill her voice with rage. "The Coalition sent that broadcast to break our spirits. They want us to lose hope and surrender. Well, I'll tell you what. It's had the opposite effect on me.

"I have a message for the Coalition. They did not kill my spirit." Her hand clenched around the comm unit, her knuckles turning white. She shouted into it, letting out all of her grief and rage. "The Union is not afraid of them. I am not afraid of them. And we will step on the Coalition's murderous necks and crush them."

The crowd erupted into a clapping, cheering frenzy. A few people whooped, and others hollered. Chills seized her joints.

Behind her, the nun whispered, "Amen."

Renewed hope charged the air. Katherine took several difficult breaths to steady herself, both against the boiling anger and the aching throughout her muscles and joints. Lori and Bindu stood close, though they did not touch her.

Unsteady legs and all, Katherine pushed herself up and managed to walk through the crowd under her own power, inclining her head to well-wishers, and those stirred enough to cry for the heads of every Coalition soldier that existed. For a moment, at least, the people of Perdition were focused again.

She hoped they did not see how near she was to collapse. Her stomach churned, and pain sent stars across her vision.

"Captain, let's head back to your quarters. I'll get engineering to re-route command functions there. That way, you don't need to be on your feet," Bindu said, her voice hesitant, almost as if she feared having her head snapped off.

"That is a sensible idea, but first, I have someone to speak with. Commander, you and Raewadee head back to OPs. Sister, would you kindly assist me to the market?"

"It would be my honor," Sister Mary Nora said.

Lori and Bindu said their good-byes before bustling to the nearest lift. Only a few moments passed before Salim's shop was in view. She dismissed the nun and pushed herself out of the chair. She walked into Salim's shop on shaky legs, ignoring the two fully-armed riot guards. The windows were missing. Many of his display stands sprawled on the floor, soaps and toiletries crushed and ground into the tiles.

"Salim," she said, her voice hard.

He turned around, broom in hand and white powder botched over his dark face and clothes. "Captain! What on earth are you doing out of hospital?"

"Is it too late?" She glared at him, truly worried that she had missed her window of opportunity. She near hated herself for having ever wavered. Never again.

He cocked his head, a quizzical look on his face.

She spoke slower. "The plan. Is it too late?"

Understanding spread over his face. He licked his lips. "What about ethics?"

"Fuck ethics."

CHAPTER ELEVEN

Katherine identified a look that she had never seen on Salim's face before: shock. His mouth opened, as though he wanted to speak, but no words came out. Finally, he forced out a word, his voice husky. "Captain?"

She thrust her chin out as far as her aching body allowed. "You said I needed to act quickly. I've been in coma, so you will pardon my tardiness. Can you still do it?"

He stared at her. Katherine could see the mental debate on his face, the corners of his mouth twitching as he thought. She couldn't fathom what he could possibly be debating. It was his idea, after all. Finally, he tipped his head to the side. "Are you certain?"

She took another step closer, hoping to intimidate him. Instead, she sneezed from the soapy floral scents around her. Her ankle rolled in the process. Losing her balance, Katherine grabbed a steel rack of slippers to keep her upright. Salim took two strides to reach a hand out to catch her but pulled back at her glare. Behind her, she heard the stomp of heavy boots, but Salim raised his hand to stop the guards from entering.

"Captain," Salim said, his voice low and steady, the way a person speaks to an injured dog.

Katherine's limbs shook, but she held on, steadying herself, mentally blocking the pain like they had taught her during training. Tears stung her eyes. The training wasn't perfect.

"You really shouldn't be standing up," Salim said in a worrisome voice that only served to annoy her. He forced a smile. "If you fall and crack your skull, Commander Windrunner will mount my head on a pike out in the docking bay."

Katherine gritted her teeth. "There aren't any pikes there."

One side of his mouth twitched upward. "I'm sure she could fabricate one for the event." He eyed her. "If I fetch you a chair, will you sit in it?"

Katherine nodded meekly. He left her there long enough to grab a chair from the front display window, a plush pink thing, and positioned it behind her. Holding on to the slipper rack, she eased herself into it. Air hissed out of it. She would have rolled her eyes if they hadn't hurt so much. She sneezed and mumbled about wishing the neutralizer still deadened some of her senses.

They stared at each other as Katherine again took several steadying breaths. In the fog of medication, she blurted out, "Why do you betray the Coalition by decoding their transmissions?"

She had not expected to ask him that. From the surprised expression on his face, neither had he. Salim crossed his arms and stared at her for a long moment. He looked past her, at the guards.

Then, he sighed, relaxing his posture, and answered in a low voice. "I don't fight them because of hate, Captain. I fight because of love. I love my home." Hardened resolve spread across his face, washing away the wistful expression. "What they are doing is wrong, and it will eventually be their downfall. The faster I can end the war, the better their chances of survival. They will never let me return, but it doesn't mean I stopped caring."

Katherine looked at him, seeing Salim in a new light. She rarely believed anything that came out of his mouth. This time, however, she knew she heard the truth. As long as she remembered why he helped her, she could trust him to not betray her. "Then you must understand why I will turn my back on the founding principles of my own people to save their lives."

He shrugged, looking unimpressed. "I think you are doing it because you are angry and want the Coalition to pay for Commander Roberts' death and for the fact they orphaned you. There is no professional justification for your actions."

Katherine clenched her hands on the seat edge until her fingers cramped. If not for the weakness of her legs, she would have stood. Instead, she glared into his eyes and said, "I will make them pay."

Salim frowned and stepped to straighten up the slipper display. He picked up three pairs of fuzzy blue footwear from the floor and hung them back on the rack. He didn't speak, which only served to annoy Katherine even more.

"Well? You put the idea in my head in the first place. Suddenly, you're squeamish about it? Let me tell you something, Salim." She growled her words. "I can force you to help me."

He stopped fiddling with his display rack and turned to look her in the eyes, his own dancing. A pleased smiled spread across his face. "Yes, you can. Would you?"

She narrowed her eyes. "I will do anything to bring the Alliance into this war on the Union's side." A chill spread through her, a mixture of knowing her words were wrong and not caring. A week before, she would not have even imagined saying them. That was before the Coalition showed their true selves. Now, she would show hers.

"Revenge is an interesting emotion. It can make a person stupid or determined. I can't work with stupid, but determined is another matter altogether. I will call my friend."

Katherine let out a small gasp; she didn't realize she had been holding her breath. She stood, her joints wishing she hadn't.

"It's not professional, and it will probably get you killed, but I will help you. For the greater good."

She inclined her head at him. "For the greater good."

With that, she gingerly made her way outside the shop. She walked past the guards, still ignoring them, eased herself into the wheelchair, and flipped the switch on the left armrest to "A" for assist. The wheelchair buzzed to life, and using a small stirring knob on the right armrest, she wheeled herself back to her quarters.

There was nothing else for it. She would bring an end to the war or die trying.

CHAPTER TWELVE

Once in the comfort of her bedroom-*cum*-command center, Katherine sprawled across her sofa while reading a data pad. The connection was slower, but it was easier to read, as opposed to leaning to view the faster, but stationary, console. A sweet, grandmother of a nurse had dropped by earlier to give her a suppresser. Katherine could have kissed the woman. The searing pain became tolerable and would remain so for twelve hours, if doctors could be trusted. A flute solo, loud enough to hear but soft enough to work to, echoed throughout her quarters.

After reassigning many of her daily reports and tasks to various members of her senior crew, she began brainstorming how to actually go about forging documents. Salim had provided detailed specifics about how Coalition reporting was done. His information matched the little experience she had, so she accepted his word at face value.

She would have reflected on how her trust in Salim had grown since their talk earlier that day, except that she didn't have enough energy for it. Her focus was on finding someone to make the documentation, not on letting the drugs suck her into a philosophical exploration of her actions.

She reached out a hand and tapped the computer console that sat where her coffee table once stood.

"Voice command activation," she said.

"Voice activated," replied the computer, in a voice that now sounded suspiciously like Ensign O'Connor.

Katherine closed her eyes and blew out a long breath, a calming technique she had learned in yoga. She did not chide herself for the apprehension. Instead, she accepted it. Embraced it.

She opened her eyes and frowned. The technique had failed to calm her. It did, however, aggravate her ribs. "Computer, I need to compile a list of Union Fleet personnel with a specific skill set."

"Please list skill sets."

She thought about that, wondering how to phrase it. Then, a thought occurred to her. "Delay list. Do we keep a record of all searches?"

"Yes."

She chewed on her lip. Mission success depended largely upon secrecy. There couldn't be records of her activities.

"Computer, please delete my search from the archives after it is completed."

"That action requires the access code of another senior officer."

She grunted, annoyed by Fleet security. Then, after thinking about the entire situation, she chuckled. The entire point of the measure was to curtail high-ranking officers abusing their authority to commit illegal acts. Like she was doing.

Katherine tapped the communications button on the console. "Francis to Windrunner."

"Windrunner here," Lori chimed a few seconds later. "What can I do for you, Captain?"

"Would you come to my quarters, please? I need another senior officer's access codes."

"Of course. Give me a few moments to get there."

Katherine leaned back on the sofa. The doctor said the next few days would be the most critical for her recovery. She pulled out the green medical pad that had wedged itself between her torso and the sofa. She read the orders, instantly yawning.

Three hours of physical therapy daily for the first week. Sessions will be broken into one-hour intervals. To ensure compliance, a therapist will be sent to retrieve patient from her quarters.

Katherine gave an indignant huff. Though, the doctor did actually know her; her refusal to follow doctors' orders was widely known. She wouldn't have been surprised if it was detailed in her medical charts somewhere.

Patient has requested Level 4 pain suppression, to be administrated every twelve hours. If patient comes to her senses, she is authorized for up to Level 1 suppression for the next three days, dropping to Level 2 for the next twenty days. Pain management requirements will be reassessed at that point.

A chill gripped her neck. Intellectually, she knew her injures were severe. However, Level 1 medications were used for those near death. The only thing higher was Level A, used in medical euthanasia. She cringed, thinking about how death had nearly knocked on her door.

A fleeting thought about joining her family flashed across her mind. She pushed it aside. Grief had no place in her life right now. Mourning could wait; the dead wouldn't care. The mission came first.

The door chimed before opening, and Lori walked in. Katherine had posted a 'Come on in' sign on her door. She didn't see any need to lock it during her regular office hours, and there were about a dozen guards in her hallway in any case.

"Good day, Katherine. You're looking well-rested."

Katherine didn't comment. Between the hurt and the guilt, she couldn't do small talk right now.

"You needed my codes?"

Katherine didn't bother sitting up; she didn't have the strength. Her insides fluttered, but she struggled to not let it show. "Yes. Can you sign in?"

Lori nodded, walking over to the coffee table-computer console hybrid. She placed her hand on the scanner and asked, in a conversational tone, "What do you need it for?"

Katherine hesitated. She had not expected Lori to ask and, thus, had no lie prepared.

Lori noticed the hesitation and pulled her hand off the

scanner, not completing the access log in. "I can't give you my authorization codes without knowing what it's for."

"I-I can't tell you what it's for." Katherine stumbled over the words. Heat rose in her cheeks, both from frustration and embarrassment. She was a rotten liar.

Lori crossed her arms.

"Damn it, Lori," Katherine snapped. "I can't tell you."

The two women stared at each other for a long moment before Lori said, "I don't need specifics."

Katherine's tension eased a little, to the delight of her sore muscles. "I am working on a project for Admiral Ortora. Secrecy is vital."

Lori paused for another moment before putting her hand back on the scanner. "Sorry, Katherine. When you hesitated, I got this idea that you were about to do something illegal to get back at the Coalition. I don't know what I was thinking."

Shame stabbed Katherine's heart, and she looked away before Lori could see it written all over her face. "It's my fault. I'm on edge."

The computer beeped, confirming that it had scanned and confirmed the commander's identification. She began typing in her access code and giving Katherine full use of the codes. "Is four hours long enough?"

"I believe so, yes," Katherine said quietly. She hated lying. It made her feel dirty inside. She tried to adjust herself, and a small, uncontrollable groan of discomfort escaped her lips.

Lori stood up and asked, "Can't they give you something stronger? I mean, you had most of your insides stitched back together. I'd figure you could get doped up good for that."

Katherine shook her head. "Stronger meds would make me a drooling idiot on the floor."

Lori headed toward the door. "That sounds pretty good. Could you ask the doc for some? Hand them over to me."

Katherine forced a smile. Lori trusted her, and she had violated that very trust. If the plan failed, she would face both Lori's professional and personal rejection. Katherine wasn't sure she could live with that end. She reminded herself it was all the more an incentive to make the plan work.

"Did you need anything before I go? Something to eat, maybe?"

"No, thanks."

Lori nodded and left the room, leaving Katherine alone with the access codes and a sinking feeling of guilt. She pushed it aside. Salim had told her she'd need to make difficult choices. A few small lies to her friends were a part of the greater good.

Katherine ran the skill search, looking for someone with sufficient technical skill to pull off forging high-level military documents. The majority of names that came up were from Intel. No surprise there. However, they were all missing one or two of the vital skills.

One name sat at the top of the list, in crimson red, with the words 'Best Match' flashing next to it. Her blood ran cold, sending a chill throughout her body. A stab of white-hot pain seared through her body when every muscle in her body clenched in reaction to the name.

Randall White. Former Fleet Master Corporal, White was serving a life sentence for the murders of eighteen men and forty women, all unregistered prostitutes. That didn't count the three hundred or so sexual assaults he had committed on both men and women. Everyone in the Union knew the name Randall White.

She double checked the skills list, hoping for a computer error. It never came. White had been in Intel. He was a genius at computer manipulation. Using a neural interface of his own design, he could hack any system and rewire it. He held double doctorates in holographic design and nano-engineering.

He was perfect for the job.

He was also criminally insane; his neural interface had destroyed key brain pathways. Perdition wasn't designed to handle dangerous offenders.

A sick feeling spread across her. She needed him.

"Computer, who is in charge of Arcon Penal Colony?"

"Mr. Jonas Star," the computer answered.

Katherine stared at the unfinished ceiling. She didn't know him. Getting a criminal like White released would need a personal connection. The problem was that the penal colonies were all run by the government. Civilians. Her contacts were Fleet.

"Computer, run a search on my background history to see if there are any overlaps between me and any Arcon staff, present or in the last twenty years."

"Running search."

Katherine had no real hopes of finding a connection, but she would be remiss in her duty without the attempt.

"There are four connections."

Katherine raised her eyebrows. Four was more than she expected. "List them."

"Rachel Wesley, currently serving as janitor. Previous connection was Fleet dorm janitor—"

"Skip. Next?"

"Michael Roberts, currently serving as the Beta Sector's Penal Colony Administrator."

Katherine blinked in surprise and sat up, wincing. She knew that name.

"Previous connection was through Commander John Roberts. He is Commander Roberts' brother."

Katherine laughed so hard it made her ribs rattle and her stomach muscles burn. She tapped her comm again. "O'Connor," she said, "I need a secure channel to Michael Roberts. He's at Arcon Penal Colony."

"Yes, Captain. It is nearly midnight there, however."

"Don't care," she snapped. "Wake him up and tell him it's important."

"Yes, Captain." The communications line closed.

Katherine struggled to her feet and shuffled to the kitchen to make coffee and perhaps a snack. She didn't want to celebrate too soon, but the odds were in her favor. If anyone could be convinced to help her, it would be John's brother. They had only met once, but that wasn't important. Their connection went beyond knowing each other. John was their connection.

She shoved an oversized mug into the small alcove in her kitchenette's wall and pressed 92—the computer code for a café au lait, jumbo. A few seconds passed before the beverage dispenser rumbled to life and began pouring her drink. She inhaled the bitter coffee smell, and her stomach growled. Katherine realized she hadn't eaten all day.

The food dispenser on the other side of her tiny kitchenette had a limited selection that the machine stored ingredients for and combined into semi-edible food. She stared at the choices and decided upon the individual banana bread. The machine flashed "3 minutes" before a countdown began. Buttery banana scent wafted from the machine.

Katherine leaned against the wall, using it to take the strain off her legs. A high-pitched chime sounded. Instinctively, she reached for the food dispenser. The chime went again. Communications, she thought. Holding her coffee in one hand, she used the other to slide across the walls to keep her balance.

She reached the table, tapped the blinking light, and collapsed into the sofa, coffee sloshing over the mug edges and to the floor.

A bald man, pale with blood-shot eyes, stared at her. "Katherine Francis."

"Yes. Thank you for taking my call, Mr. Roberts—"

He waved her off. "I hate to be rude to someone who was my brother's best friend, but I'm tired. What can I do for you?"

"I need Randall White for a week."

His eyes grew wide. "I did not hear that right."

"You did. I need him on my station for a week. I can... trade." The last word stuck in her throat, but she forced it out. The notion of trading a human being sickened her, though not as much as bringing a convicted killer to Perdition.

"Captain, there is no possible way that I can authorize the expense and transport of the most notorious criminal in recent history to enjoy a furlough at your—"

"It's for the war," Katherine blurted.

Michael stopped, his mouth still opened from having formed a soundless word. He stared at her over the video screen and narrowed his eyes. "How?"

She stared back, making no attempt to answer him. Her slip had already cost her enough. Knowledge was too precious a commodity to sling around when her career was on the line. Hell, her life probably was, too.

Michael grunted. Then, he said, "John and I talked before he... He said that you had a new plan to help with the war. He didn't give me details, but he was excited about it."

Katherine didn't move. She did not want to give away that this had nothing to do with the drone plan. It would be a good cover, of course. She worked to keep her face a blank mask, hoping that Michael's own thoughts would paint himself into the position to help her.

"He also told me you ordered a new industrial fabricator. We've been without one for three months now. The government seems to think the war is more important than replacing prison door latches after a riot."

She licked her lips. Katherine did not like this.

"I can have White to you in fifty hours if you direct that fabricator to come our way."

She fought off the initial "no" and moved to considering the offer. The shortage of fabricators already slowed down Perdition repairs, not to mention battle damaged ships. The drone plan moved along slowly because of the parts and supplies shortage. The new fabricator would help them recycle their scrap metal into new material.

"I'm not willing to do that. Besides, it's a Class Eight fabricator. It's meant to be tethered in space to recycle a ship's hull. It's a power hog."

"I'm not willing to send White without significant compensation for the effort of dragging his ass off the colony."

Katherine considered that for a moment. "We do have a portable smaller one, the size of a two-seater shuttle. It's generally used for wiring, furniture, security doors, that sort of thing.

I could loan it to you for a week."

He laughed, the rich laugh that reminded her of John. Her hands shook, and she clenched them, fighting off the quiver in her soul. "It would take us days to get your machine fitted to make it useful. Six months."

"Three," she hammered back, trying to wipe away the image of Bindu's ire over that.

"Deal. Fifty hours, then."

She nodded her agreement to the terms. Costly, but not overly so. Their focus was ship upgrades anyway, and they needed the larger fabricator. Besides, they had a mid-sized one that could handle the tiny details.

"One week, Captain. After that, I want him back on my colony or dead. Either is fine. I'm not fussy."

She inclined her head at him.

Michael grew somber. "Captain, John talked about you. He had a lot of respect for you."

A lump formed in Katherine's throat. "And I him."

"I want that fabricator." He leaned forward, and a small growl entered his voice. "And I want the Coalition bastards dead." With that, the feed went black.

Katherine leaned against the sofa's back for a moment before collapsing down to one side. She abandoned the banana bread, its sweet smell now nauseating. She had used her best friend's death to get her own way.

For the greater good.

As long as you don't get caught.

CHAPTER THIRTEEN

The further down the report she read, the more Katherine's agitation grew. Her drone plan had passed muster with the three key departments—engineering, communications, and fabrication. That alone was a milestone; those three rarely agreed on anything. Unfortunately, the universal problem with the plan was the shortage of parts. It didn't help that Katherine lied to engineering, stating that they had been ordered to give their smallest fabricator to a penal colony.

She couldn't request a new fabricator so soon after trading hers away. In a few months, yes. Right now? It would raise too many awkward questions; questions she was not ready to answer. Katherine pondered asking Admiral Ortora. As usual, she dismissed the thought almost as fast as it popped into her mind. Though loathed to admit it, Katherine had begun seeing the world through Salim's eyes. If she contacted the Admiral, she'd have to recount her plan. And that would end it.

No, bringing the Alliance into the war would level the playing field and might even bring about a peace settlement. Nothing could compromise that. She'd have to find another way.

Her door chimed, and seconds later, it slid open. No one stood in the doorway, though the scent of freshly-toasted *something* along with buttery cinnamon hit her. There was a bit of clanging, and Salim stepped in front of the doorway balancing a covered platter. Her eyes widened.

"Salim, is that food?" Her stomach growled with hope.

Therapy had been first thing in the morning. The pain made it impossible to extract herself from her sofa to find breakfast. She could have called for help, but her pride stood in the way.

"Waffles." He shot her a toothy grin before walking into her quarters, toward the kitchenette. "Not just waffles, Captain. *Real* waffles. Made with real flour. And real eggs, from an actual duck. I made them this morning."

She wanted to get a better look at what he was doing. However, her sore joints refused to cooperate. "Real waffles? Not reconstituted soy protein and algae paste?"

He left the platter in the kitchenette and returned with a plate and a steaming mug of coffee, by the bitter scent of it. "A shipment came in last night, and it contained organic waffle mix, Quebec maple syrup, direct from Earth, I might add, duck eggs, and back bacon. It was payment for a favor."

Katherine's mouth watered. After three months of instant meals and field rations, the notion of real food threatened to bring tears of joy to her eyes. "Thank you."

She accepted it, careful not to drop the knife and fork that sank in the luxurious maple syrup. Eating while lying down was a talent she lacked.

"Do you need help sitting up?" Salim asked.

She glared at him, though her tone was casual. "It wouldn't help. I had my first round of physiotherapy this morning. I couldn't sit up if I tried. You'd think modern medicine would have found a better way to heal injuries."

"Time heals all wounds. Isn't that the saying?"

She shook her fork at him. "If it's old enough to have a saying, it's an outdated medical practice."

Katherine cut off a small corner and dipped the waffle into the puddle of melting butter and syrup. Then, a thought crossed her mind. "It's not poisoned, is it?"

Salim let out a loud laugh and took up the chair across from her. "Oh Captain, if I wanted to kill you, you'd be dead already."

"How comforting." The scary thing was she believed him. Katherine's food-filled fork suspended for a moment before hunger won, and she stuffed it into her mouth. The food was divine, sweet and fluffy, and just plain real. "Why did you bring me waffles? And don't lie. Something's up."

Salim leaned back and crossed his hands. "We've hit a snag."

Katherine used her fork to wave him on. "I've gotten Randall White out of prison. Surely it can't be a worse snag than trying to accomplish that."

"I suppose it would depend upon your point of view. For this Randall of yours to successfully graft the documents and images we need, several things are required. Retina scans. Hand imprint patterns. Not to mention six data pads encrypted with recent Coalition security passwords."

Katherine delayed taking the next bite. She tipped her head to face him as best as she could, pain stabbing at her neck. "As I recall, that was your responsibility."

He inclined his head. "I know someone who can provide all of these."

She narrowed her eyes at him. She didn't like bringing people into this. Too many were already tainted with a little knowledge. If her steps were ever retraced, there would be a mountain of evidence and a flashing sign pointing in her direction. "Trustworthy?"

Salim shifted, uncomfortable. "Without question. We have a history together."

Katherine didn't like how he wasn't looking her in the eye. "Then where's the snag?"

"Payment."

Katherine nodded. That didn't surprise her. She had some budgetary funds she could direct toward "security" purchases. "How much?"

Salim cleared his throat. "She wants to trade, actually."

"I've already given away a fabricator." Katherine put the final bite of waffle into her mouth and chewed. What could she offer? They were low on medical supplies and food. Hell, they were low on generally everything, except weapons. That gave her a little sinking feeling. No, she corrected herself. He'd never ask her for weapons. "Then what does your friend want?"

Salim took a deep breath. "Fifteen Station-grade warheads and a shield regenerator."

Katherine snorted before bursting into a fit of laughter that sent searing pain from her ribcage. The laughter cut off just as fast as it had begun. She pressed a hand against her side and winced, struggling to control herself. A few snickers escaped her lips.

She looked at Salim, who was not laughing. "Seriously, what does she want?"

Salim looked her in the eyes, his face cold and hard. "Fifteen Station-grade warheads and a shield regenerator."

CHAPTER FOURTEEN

Katherine stared at Salim in disbelief. "I must have heard you wrong because I'm sure you asked me to hand over warheads, the largest size we have I might add, to a stranger."

"Oh, she isn't a stranger. She's a former business associate of mine."

"Do not insult my intelligence," she snapped. Katherine slid her breakfast plate to the floor, the metal fork clanging against the hard plastic plate before hitting the carpet.

Salim remained silent as she dragged herself into a semi-seated position. White light sparkled in her vision.

"Captain, I understand your reluctance."

"You understand?" Katherine shook her head, grimacing. God, when would her body feel like her own again? "No, Salim you don't understand. You are asking me to hand over one of our most protected technologies to the black market. Why not call up the scavengers and gangs and give them the tech, because that's pretty much what we're doing here."

Salim snorted. "Tell me you are not that naive."

That took her by surprise. Her voice lowered to a whisper when she asked, "What do you mean?"

"There is a war going on. One that your side is losing, I might add. This sector is littered with pieces of Union ships. Scavengers have been selling all kinds of parts off your wrecks to Red Alert and a dozen other gangs. That includes your precious warheads."

Katherine lifted her chin defiantly. "We never leave our

ships behind."

"You do when the entire battle fleet's been blown into tiny pieces."

Her mouth snapped shut. Three engagements at the beginning of the war had been complete annihilations. Perdition had sent their salvagers to gather scrap from one of the battles, but nothing remained. "We assumed the Coalition took them."

"The Coalition would rather be paid for salvage rights than bother gathering outdated technology."

Pride stung her heart. The Union of Planets, with their Ethics Laws and fine words, lagged behind in military technology. Their leaders were too bent on peaceful negotiations and placating the core civilian population to divert funding into weapon and ship development. While her family died, while John was killed, the Union did nothing but wine and dine diplomats from independent worlds: worlds which had no desire to declare war on the Coalition.

"If our weapons are so outdated, why would your friend even want them?"

He gave her a small, apologetic smile. "An outdated warhead is still better than no warhead, Captain. Your people believe in modular design, making your ammunition useful in many situations. Union missiles are highly prized on the market."

Embarrassment washed over her. On an intellectual level, she understood. Of course there was a black market, an underground of illegal goods. Every civilization had one. This was simply the first time she had been faced with it.

Katherine frowned at that and relaxed her muscles so that her head sank back into her pillows. "The black market doesn't really touch us on Perdition. I forgot about it, to be honest." She looked back at him. "It doesn't touch us." She tried to keep her tone casual. Confident.

"Captain, I spent over an hour convincing my friend that talking to me about smuggling wouldn't get her arrested. The Union might go down in history as being the first people to entirely eliminate smuggling within their borders."

Katherine eyed him for a moment, unsure if his words were truth or flattery. She decided they were a mixture of both. Perdition was Fleet-run, so the black market rarely stepped onboard. Sure, occasionally contraband was found, but it wasn't common, not like on the civilian-run docking ports elsewhere in the sector. "I still can't give away warheads."

Salim's eyes widened. "You honestly don't know what Union missiles are used for, do you?"

"I assume to blow things up."

Salim rolled his eyes. "I'd like to get my hands on your Intelligence people. They don't seem to be too bright."

Katherine gave a soft chuckle.

"Union warheads can be turned into a number of things. They can be armed with all manner of biogenetic tips—"

Katherine gasped. She opened her mouth, not even sure she *could* respond to that, but Salim lifted a hand to silence her.

"Generally, people buy them to break them down and make smaller munitions."

Katherine cocked her head at him, confused. "That makes no sense."

"On the contrary. A person can make forty-two smart mines from one Union warhead. With a small amount of skill and a pair of needle-nose pliers, a person can reprogram the detonation and guidance sequences. With that, you have enough firepower to discourage a small ground army from storming your personal stronghold."

"Smart mines are easy to build, though." She pondered her words for a moment. "Oh, but detonation and guidance programs are not. That's the real reason for wanting the warheads. Union guidance programs are even better than the Alliance's. One warhead is useless when defending a complex on the ground. However, a perimeter of smart mines..." Her voice trailed off.

She shook her head. "I can't give away fifteen warheads. Not to mention a shield generator, too."

"It's warheads or back to the drone plan."

Indignation filled her voice. "I'm still going ahead with the drone plan."

Salim crossed his arms. "And how is that working for you, Captain? I hear the shortage of parts has pretty much stopped the entire enterprise."

"Clearly, I need to retrain my crew to make sure you hear less." She took a deep breath. "Warheads are big. Someone will notice they are gone. And a shield generator is out of the question. We only have two, and our main one is flaky. I might as well hang a sign inviting the Coalition to attack Perdition."

"I'm sure she will negotiate."

Katherine stared at her unfinished ceiling and listened to the pipes bang and shake. She thought about John and what he would do. He'd say not to trust Salim. That didn't stop him from throwing himself in the line of fire to save the shopkeeper. John liked to talk big about violating the rules, but he supported them as much as she did. Katherine thought of her family, executed on sector-wide vid feeds. She thought of the Perdition inhabitants, Fleet and clergy and civilian, all desperate for an end to the war. They needed the Alliance. John would have understood exceptions.

"Why are you smiling?" Salim asked.

Katherine snorted. "I was thinking about Commander Roberts and his plan for ending the war with the Coalition."

"Suicide bombers." A contemplative look came over Salim's face. "It could work in a pinch, as long as the bombs aren't attached to me."

Katherine frowned and tapped her fingers against the sofa's edge. Joking aside, she knew what was going to happen. "There's no point in me pretending I'm not going to do this, because we both know I am. So, give me one reason why I should."

Salim gave one of his signature non-committal shrugs, the ones that annoyed Katherine to her core. "If you aren't interested in bringing the Alliance into the war, I can leave. I have nothing invested in this little venture."

Perhaps it was the tone of his voice, but fury swept through

Katherine. She pushed herself up, struggling and wincing, angered by his manipulative words. Once sitting up, she leaned toward him. "That is a lie."

Surprise flickered in his eyes.

She pressed on. "We both know I don't believe your little businessman facade. It's cute and funny, and generally harmless. Until now. You want me to hand over enough firepower to destroy a ground attack force. You *will* tell me why."

They glared at each other. Katherine clenched her jaw. She would not back down. The time for cute deception had passed.

Salim broke the stare first. A long sigh escaped him. "All right. My friend is Tobi Rowe."

Katherine gasped in surprise. "*The* Tobi Rowe?"

A smug, prideful smile spread across Salim's face. "It's comforting that you know my security records inside and out. She was my apprentice, and the Coalition destroyed her career when they came after me. The difference is that I tucked my tail between my legs and came to the Union for protection. Tobi was still young and full of piss and vinegar."

"Why does she want the weapons?"

"She plans to nuke the Coalition until it's little more than a dust cloud."

Katherine clicked her tongue against the roof of her mouth. She didn't feel particularly bad about that idea. "Giving to Tobi would be like helping a sister in arms?"

Salim shrugged and said, "More like a freedom fighter. Or, terrorist, depending upon who you ask."

Katherine nodded and took the data pad wedged between the sofa and her back. She eased herself down on the pillow once more and tapped out several sentences. Then, she opened a communications line to Lori.

"Windrunner here."

"Have Munitions package nine small warheads for interstellar shipping. The orders are coming to your console now." She looked at Salim, her gaze meant to challenge him on the number. He merely inclined his in agreement.

Lori remained silent for a moment before asking, "Who is Admiral Salem? I don't know that name."

Katherine tensed. Admiral Salem was Katherine's childhood cat, whose name she forged on the orders. "It's a need-to-know name."

"If I'm giving out weapons, I need to know."

Katherine took a deep breath to keep her tone calm. "Commander, I need you to process this request."

Another pause. "These orders don't say where the warheads are going."

Katherine pushed down the uneasy feeling in her gut. "That's correct. I will personally be overseeing the shipping."

"Without proper shipping instructions—"

"Commander Windrunner, I gave you a direct order. Is that understood?" Katherine clenched her jaw.

A moment passed before Lori said in a resigned tone, "I'll notify you when it's done."

Katherine cut the feed. A sickly feeling spread inside her. Yet another bread crumble of evidence to bury her.

Katherine turned to Salim and said, "We don't use many small warheads, so those nine won't be missed. I'll direct two shield batteries to the cargo bay as well for shipment. I can't give a shield generator, but the batteries are the most difficult component to come by. If Tobi can pull apart a warhead, she can make a basic generator from the batteries."

Salim rose from his chair. "I believe she will find this acceptable."

"Not so fast. Tell her I want an industrial fabricator."

Salim gave her a wide, toothy grin. "Captain, I like the way you think."

Exhaustion crept over her. She didn't smile. Giving weaponry to anyone non-Fleet was illegal. Union core government had an entire department of bureaucrats who did nothing but investigate corruption in all its forms. If Lori did note the transfer in the logs, eventually someone would find it. Arranging this entire plan was becoming more and more complicated. Katherine began to wonder if she was even the good guy anymore.

Nevertheless, she needed the Alliance in the war on the Union's side. Tobi Rowe had everything she needed to bring that about: scanners, patterns, encrypted pads, security codes. She might even get a fabricator out of it.

She'd worry about her conscience later.

CHAPTER FIFTEEN

Katherine stood at the south docking bay and waited. Flanking her were eight security guards dressed in full riot gear: black tunic and trousers with multiple pockets, thick-soled but silent boots, and black helmets with tinted visors to protect both their faces and identities.

Of course, these guards were armed. Weapons were strictly banned from the common areas on Perdition. Only Station law enforcement wore them; Fleet personnel didn't even wear their side arms in the civilian areas. However, Katherine would not accept custody of the likes of Randall White without armed guards surrounding him at all times. To mitigate any strife or uncomfortable questions, Katherine personally saw to every detail of White's arrival. She even arranged for his transport ship to dock at the southern bay where only dignitaries, celebrities, and other security risk people normally arrived. If a serial killer didn't count as a security risk, Katherine didn't know who possibly could.

The metal floor beneath her vibrated, and she heard the distant, but distinct, clang of the docking anchors grabbing hold of a ship on the other side of the blast doors. It would still be several minutes before he'd be brought out. Nerves caused her breakfast to slosh around in her stomach. At least the pain was less today, though she decided that was due to not having yet had her morning physiotherapy session as opposed to any real healing.

Details concerning Patricia's imminent arrival flashed across her thoughts. In a couple of weeks, she'd be standing in one of the other docking areas, waiting for her wife to step off a transport. They might even speak to each other.

Katherine pushed those worries down to the base of her feet. She did not have time for personal indulgences. At any moment, the most notorious criminal in decades, if not centuries, was stepping onto her station. She needed to stay focused.

Heavy footsteps and labored breathing caught her attention, and she snapped her head around, as did the guards. Eight pulse rifles rose in unison in the direction of the sound.

Color drained from Salim's bronze features for a brief moment before an easy smile spread across his face. He raised his hands. Slowly.

"You're late," Katherine said blandly before turning back to face the doors.

Around her, pulse chambers whined as safeties went back on the rifles. She heard a few more footsteps before Salim stood at her side. "I apologize for being late, Captain. You failed to mention to the rather large contingent of security guards at the corridor entrance that I was the person you were waiting for."

"I'm quite sure I was clear. Perhaps they didn't trust you." She gave him a knowing grin. "Have any idea why Perdition security would be suspicious of you?"

He gave her a toothy smile. "I have no idea, Captain."

One of the security guards grunted. She glared at him long enough to ensure the silent warning would not be mistaken. Bringing White to the station served as the key step in bringing the Alliance into the conflict. With the Alliance on their side, the Union would win the war. She was too close to have a faceless security guard disrespect Salim, her only chance at making the entire plan work.

"You look rather spry this morning, Captain," Salim observed.

"I haven't been tortured by Dr. Chan yet. I convinced him to push up the session long enough to let me come here."

Salim cocked an eyebrow. "How?"

She leaned toward him, careful not to lose her balance. "A box of chocolates."

Salim roared with laughter, and even Katherine let out a little chuckle. It had been too long since anyone had laughed around her. When the moment passed, however, the silence seemed all the more strained. True happiness would not exist for a long time yet.

They stood in silence for the next several minutes until a green light above the metal blast doors began flashing.

"They're coming," Katherine said. A cold sweat engulfed her, even as her cheeks grew warm. She gulped down the nerves as best as she could.

When Randall White walked through the doors, shackled and accompanied by four heavily-armed guards, Katherine fought against her screaming instincts to grab the nearest weapon and shoot him dead. She didn't realize how tensely she held herself until her muscles began protesting. She took a deep, calming breath and stepped forward.

"I am Captain Katherine Francis. Welcome to Perdition Docking Port."

The lead guard flipped up her tinted visor before offering to shake Katherine's hand. "Pleased to meet you, Captain. I'm Master Corporal LeBlanc, in charge of the prisoner transport."

Katherine looked down at the woman and smiled. She couldn't have been more than a meter and a half tall and, if Katherine were to guess, fifty-five kilos at best. Anyone that little in charge of a dangerous prisoner must be one tough character. Katherine didn't want to find out how tough.

"Did you receive our recommended security requirements for White?"

Katherine nodded. "I've had one of our dignitary quarters converted according to your recommendations." Under any other circumstances, she would have insisted on having him deep in the midst of the containment area. However, it would be difficult to explain why a convicted murderer would need computer access, a holo-generator, and classified Intel reports.

Katherine dismissed her nagging conscience. A few lies and broken rules were nothing in the grand scheme of peace.

LeBlanc handed Katherine a key. "This will deactivate the magnetic locks on his cuffs. We'll be back to pick him up in seven days."

Katherine palmed the key, the metal, cold against her skin. "A week will be plenty. Sergeant Prasad, please escort Mr. White to his guest quarters."

"Yes, Captain," Prasad said gruffly before taking two long strides to get in front of White. The guards exchanged nods before Prasad turned, White following. The other Perdition guards circled White, and they walked down the corridor. Katherine licked her lips and asked Leblanc, "Is it true that he's really fixed?"

The master corporal shrugged. "I can only repeat what the doctors have told us. Once he stopped using his neural interface, his empathy pathways grew back. He doesn't talk much anymore, but he'll do whatever you ask him to do. I wouldn't trust him, though. It's important to remember that he killed a lot of people and hurt even more. He hasn't been 'cured' long enough for me to trust him."

Katherine nodded in agreement, though she asked, "How long would he need to be cured for you to trust him?"

"I doubt his life span would reach that length," she said without smiling. "Good luck, Captain. Your project must be important to need White's help."

"It is," Katherine said, this time the one not smiling. She waited for the guards to exit back through the blast doors. She took a deep breath and turned. Time to meet her mass murderer.

CHAPTER SIXTEEN

The irony of housing a serial killer in Perdition's dignitary's room did not escape Katherine. As she walked down the long, abandoned corridor leading to the Ambassador Suite, Katherine hesitated before turning the corner. So much had happened and all too fast. It took her a moment to center herself. The uncertainty did not shake her resolve, however. She was already too far in.

The next corridor was a stark contrast to all others on the docking port. Where non-slip metal covered station walkways, this elite section's floor sported clean, dark blue carpet. Instead of metal walls covered with lights, real honest-to-God wood paneling covered the walls in a rich mahogany. The normally stark walls sported colorful artwork from the Union's most prominent artists. Where no one generally stood, five guards dressed in black held staggered positions throughout the area.

Fit for a king.

She had given the orders for security to clear and scan the entire section, plus the two decks above and below. No one in OPs knew what she was planning or who had arrived. It was her goal to keep it that way. That was the purpose of the guards.

Katherine inclined her head to the three guards adjacent to White's door. The shortest of the group, Prasad returned the gesture. The other guards loomed over both Prasad and Katherine and remained still. She found herself looking up at them, awed by their height. Katherine was a tall woman, but these men hit two full meters and were nearly as wide. Again, she wondered at Leblanc's skills as a special operations guard for Intel with her almost laughable height.

Katherine rounded the corner and stared. Salim stood in the corridor, his body pressed against the wall, his limbs spread wide apart. A black-clad guard pointed a pulse rifle at him.

"Ah, Captain, finally," Salim said, exasperated.

She sighed, frustration mounting. If she didn't return to her quarters soon, no doubt the doctor would put a full scale priority alert out to find her. She didn't have the time to fool around with Salim.

"Why aren't you inside?" she demanded. Salim's entire purpose was to help get White started and to review the technical side of things. She wasn't an expert on holographic tech and document creation. Besides, the ache in her back was beginning to rage, and soon she wouldn't be able to stand up.

"Because this fine, Union guard threatened to turn me into a smudge on the floor if I stepped inside without your permission."

While Katherine could not see through the polarized face shield of the helmet, the guard's body language clearly said he waited for confirmation.

"Salim is permitted to enter and exit at will for the duration of our guest's," she choked on the word, "visit."

"Yes, Captain," he replied and lowered his rifle and stepped aside, allowing Salim to pass. Katherine gave credit to Salim; he did not seem rumpled by the misunderstanding. He smiled brightly at the guard and trotted up to her.

"Thank you for the timely rescue, Captain. Where did you find them? If the entire Union fleet was trained like that one, your people would have already invaded Coalition territory." His smile remained though Katherine noted it did not reach his eyes.

"You have your secrets, Salim. I have mine."

"I've always liked you, Captain." He laughed, an easy, friendly sound, and they took the last several steps to the Ambassador Suite in silence. Katherine had been uncertain about the guard situation when she first agreed to bring White to Perdition. Thankfully, she knew the identities of three Intel operatives on Perdition who worked on the security force; something not even the head of security knew. She pulled a couple of strings to get the names of the rest from the ships docked at port. It was not an ideal situation to trust strangers, but Intel operatives had a reputation.

Seeing how they'd reacted so far, she felt her gamble had been worth it. If Salim couldn't get through, no one would.

The three guards at the door stepped aside as Katherine approached. One rang the doorbell for her. The doors slid open, and two burly men blocked the entrance.

"Soldiers," she said and then took a step forward. They parted and allowed her to walk in. "Salim is granted full access to our guest."

"Yes, Captain," they replied in unison.

She eyed the room, its opulence a frustrating wraith, an echo of a pre-war Union of Planets, where dignitaries came to be wined and dined. Now, it housed a criminal.

White stood in the far corner, staring out the window at the star-spotted view. He wore simple black trousers with a brown shirt, the kind that remained stylish yet functional regardless of the era. He had a small bald spot on the back of his head.

Katherine fought against her nerves. She couldn't determine if her anxiety came from the mission itself, or a fear that White might hurt her, like the countless others. Regardless, she took a deep breath and asked, ""Have you read the requirements for this job?"

He continued to stare out the window, but he nodded. "You want me to create a number of documents meant to simulate a covert operation taking place in Alliance territory by the Coalition. You'll need holo-vids, retina scans, hand scans, and signatures integrated into the documents' security features, all which need to pass a rigorous inspection."

"That's correct." Katherine paused long enough for the cold chill to leave her body. The laundry list of illegal activities bothered her enough without having them recited by a cold, calculating voice. "Can you do it?"

He looked at her, his eyes dead of emotion. She shuddered at the lack of humanity in his stare. "I wouldn't be here if I couldn't."

She straightened her back as best she could. It hurt. A lot. "Let me put it to you this way. Will you do it?"

A small smile flickered on his face. "I wouldn't be here if I wouldn't help. I hate to travel. I get space sick." He turned back to the window, crossing his arms.

"Salim Tobin is a..." she struggled to find the word, growing more uncomfortable by the passing second.

White turned around again to face her. "*Business associate* is the usually acceptable term." He looked at Salim and said, "Though I've heard that spy and assassin are more correct labels for your varied business interests."

Katherine glanced at Salim, whose face betrayed no true emotion. Sure, his face held that mildly amused look he often got, but it didn't light up his features the way true amusement did. She filed away that look, in case she needed to read him in the future.

Salim stretched out his arms in an exaggerated fashion. "How thrilling. They let the criminally insane read confidential Intel files during their incarceration." He shook his head, a small frown on his face. "No wonder your people are losing this war."

White took a step toward Salim, and Katherine tensed immediately. Even if there were several guards nearby, she did not want this first meeting to devolve into chaos. She had too much riding on their success and too little patience for a testosterone contest.

"Enough," she warned, her tone low. "We're here to work."

White didn't look at her, his eyes remained fixed on Salim's. "Obviously you haven't been reading the latest prison newsletters. Once I stopped using my neural interface, my brain healed itself, with the help of nanosurgery. I am cured. You are still a spy."

Salim chuckled. "You might've fooled the penal system, but you haven't fooled me." He glanced at Katherine, who cocked an eyebrow expectantly at him. "We're annoying the dear Captain, who can make both of our lives quite miserable. Shall we get to the business?"

Katherine stepped to the side long enough to watch Salim lead White to the computer console. While White seemed uninterested, he acquiesced in coming to the station. He also listened intently when Salim listed the basic Coalition security features that needed to be implemented in the documents. White made additional comments that, while Katherine didn't understand what they were talking about, seemed to impress Salim. The technical talk of the meeting increased exponentially as both men grew excited about the task in front of them.

Katherine took her cue and walked toward the exit. She looked over her shoulder one last time. Regardless of whether White was cured or not, she was leaving the fate of the entire Fleet in the hands of an assassin and a psychotic.

CHAPTER SEVENTEEN

Three days later, Katherine dragged herself back to the Ambassador section of Perdition. She used the lift's walls as a back support, as the small chamber hummed its way through its horizontal path to the plushest and most heavily secured areas on the station, except for Engineering, Weapons Storage, Ops, and the brig, of course. Her insides twisted and knotted with anticipation. The initial draft of the forgery documents awaited her inspection.

They were ahead of schedule; she had not expected any results for another day. Time seemed to slip by faster since Salim and White began working. Katherine could almost hear the ticking of old-fashioned clocks, reminding her that the window of opportunity was closing fast. Not to mention that Patricia was now en route to the station.

Katherine sucked in a breath of stale, recycled air. Guilt stabbed at her, but she pushed it aside. Patricia would not approve, but she never needed to know. Her opinion mattered little when the fate of the entire Union swung in the balance. Logic agreed. Her conscience did not.

The lift jolted to a halt. She sighed in relief; her eyes did not well up. The torturous therapy clearly was working. Still, her first steps out of the lift were slow and hesitant. After the review, Katherine hoped to spend an hour in OPs to test her stability and progress. Lying around her quarters benefitted the plan, but she ached to get back to work and put the accident behind her. In fact, she ached to put everything behind her: the war, the death, the compromises.

She was grateful for the near-empty corridor. It allowed her to walk at her own slow pace without eyes full of pity meeting her own. She refused to meet White while in a wheelchair, even if that was what she needed. So, slow and tentative was the only alternative.

When she turned the final corner, two guards nodded their greeting, her image mirrored in their polarized face shields. She inclined her head in reply but frowned to herself at having lost a guard. Private Winsor's ship left that morning for the front with Winsor on it. There hadn't been enough time to replace him yet.

The guard nearest the metal door tapped the wall panel, and the doors slid open, smooth and soundless except for the whisper of air in motion. Katherine stepped inside the room, her boots sinking a touch into the plush carpet. Salim, sporting a bright yellow shirt underneath a grey, button-up cardigan, stood next to the computer console, several pads in hand. White, on the other hand, still wore his prison-issue clothing and stood cross-armed at the window, staring out at the endless stream of stars. She'd not interacted with him much, true, but he seemed to do that a lot.

"Ah, Captain, I'm glad you could join us so quickly. We have significant progress to report," Salim said before motioning to the guards. "Progress our friends may not need to hear about."

Katherine pondered his words for a moment, looking between him and White. Injured, she did not want to be left alone with White in the room. True, Salim would be there, but he was older than her. White was just past thirty, and his experience in covert OPs had made him a valuable member of Intel. It also made him a killer. Caution was prudent.

However, she was committing a terrorist activity, punishable by life imprisonment in her own territory and punishable by death within Coalition borders. She trusted these guards with basic secrets only. She didn't even trust her own people with the full knowledge of her actions, let alone these strangers. The fewer who knew, the better.

"Please wait outside," she said to the guards. Sergeant Prasad hesitated before nodding his head and stepping out of the room. The others followed. Once the door whooshed closed behind them, Katherine turned back to Salim. "Well?"

He stepped over to the computer console and gestured for her to follow. The table adjacent to the console had several dozen pads spread across it. Six Coalition pads sat at the top of the table, evenly ordered next to the chaotic mess of Union data pads. "I think we have it, Captain. Here." Salim handed her a Union pad. "I haven't uploaded the full details yet. I wanted to check it all over with you first. It'll take you around six hours to review the work, but I think you'll be satisfied with it."

Katherine flipped through several screens on the pad, a transcript of falsified transmissions between top Coalition leaders. "How are you certain the data will be correct?"

"I based the core program on several Intel documents and holo-vids." He shot her a toothy grin. "It also doesn't hurt that I went to school with the Minister of Information and Dissimulation."

Katherine snorted, surprising herself. "You never mentioned that."

Salim shot her an injured, but playful, look. "You never asked."

"I'll never make the same mistake again, if that makes you more comfortable."

He beamed. "Yes, thank you."

"All right, so I'm a Coalition admiral. Let's look this over," she said, grabbing a pad from the middle of the pile.

"Why did you pick from the middle?"

She cocked an eyebrow at Salim. "If someone is offering evidence of something that seems unbelievable, shouldn't all the data stand up to scrutiny and not just the one being handed by the informant?"

Salim's smile reminded her of the ones her father used to give whenever she did something that made him proud. A mixture of self-pride and nostalgic sadness washed over her. She would never impress her father again in this life. He had been a career peacekeeper all over the Union, including Pious III for thirty-seven years before signing up for the Fleet. He went to Outpost 47 to train greenhorn security officers, two weeks before the Coalition blew it into little pieces. At least, he wasn't alone now in whatever afterlife existed for old warriors.

She shook off the thought and looked up to see a confused look at Salim's face. She loosened her grip on the pad and turned back to it, randomly flipping to different screens and sections. Her father would not have approved, but he would have supported her. She scanned battle plans filled with such detail that she silently questioned if they were in fact real ones. She wouldn't have put it past Salim.

Meeting transcripts matching the encrypted holo-vids would be the most difficult and the most crucial to reproduce. "Are the holo-vids ready?"

White nodded and walked to the console. He keyed something into the computer and a meter high projection appeared over the desk. Chills went through Katherine when the Coalition military symbol flashed on the screen. She took a deep breath, attempting to quell her nerves. They faded away to fascination when the holo-vid appeared.

Vice-Admiral Ada Northmoor: Is the recorder working?

(Senior Clerk Isabella Rosco spends 26.7 seconds at the computer console on the far left table): Yes, Admiral. It's recording correctly.

(Vice-Admiral Ada Northmoor spends 4.2 seconds drinking coffee from a self-heating thermos): Call the rest of the committee in.

The transcripts and the holo-vids matched perfectly. At random, Katherine slowed down the playback and watched the time counter. The time stamps matched to the micro-millisecond. Easy enough to do when transcribing an actual recording; virtually impossible when using pieced-together and fragmented video from various sources. The timings, the reimaging, everything needed to the perfect.

Here, in front of her, was perfection. Her heart fluttered in her chest. She looked at Salim, unable to control the awe in her voice. “How did you do this?”

“Mr. White was the key,” he said, tipping his head in the man’s direction. White remained at the window. He did not look back.

“How much of this information is falsified?”

White looked away. “Only 3.6 percent.”

Katherine cocked an eyebrow at Salim, who gave her a toothy grin. “Like I said, I have friends in interesting places.”

Katherine only offered a small smile, a difficulty considering her excitement. She did not need them to see her beaming. “I’ll review everything right away. But, well done.”

She took a deep breath, letting the soft hint of victory soothe her aching joints. The war might actually end. She might actually succeed.

As long as you don’t get caught.

CHAPTER EIGHTEEN

With a slight skip in her step, Katherine made her way to OPs. She didn't bother to hide her grin. Everyone seemed to associate it with her return to work, and she had no desire to change that thought.

"Captain!" O'Connor shouted over the hum and buzz of OPs. He was the first to pound his hands together when Katherine entered through the side doors. Three tiers of personnel broke into applause a second later. Heat rose in her cheeks, but she lifted her chin high. If they cheered for a successful entrance into OPs, she wondered what they would do when the Alliance joined the war.

Katherine corrected her thinking and, likewise, brought the applause to a halt with a firm but polite gesture. Overconfidence was a failing. She needed to control the urge to get ahead of herself. "Thank you. It's good to be back."

"I suppose you want this back."

"Yes, please, Second in Command, Commander Windrunner."

The woman beamed.

Katherine could feel both the joy of Lori's promotion and the grief of John's death. She sucked in a breath of air, steadied herself and gingerly, walked down the short set of stairs to her workstation. She tried not to use the railing, but her legs wobbled, and it was either hold on or fall. That would not have been a triumphant return.

"It's good to have you back," Commander Williams said, smiling at her from his seat at Tactical.

Katherine nodded. She struggled to plaster an answering smile on her face, thinking about all the things she'd been doing behind her staff's collective back. None of them would forgive her if they found out. Then again, the opinion of Lori and the others would be the least of her worries if her plan were found out. Still, it stung knowing how she was betraying friendships and trust.

"Captain, are you all right?"

Katherine looked up at Windrunner and forced another smile. "Yes. I haven't been back here since the transmission," she said, lowering her voice. She looked at John's old station, now Lori's. "It's a bit lonely without Commander Roberts."

Lori pressed her lips together and nodded. Then, she leaned forward and whispered, "John's mother sent me a few messages, asking after you. She thinks the world of you."

Katherine took a long, deep breath, letting it out slowly. "I've known her almost as long as I've known—" she swallowed, "him. She was at my wedding, you know."

"Well, Patricia will be on the station soon."

A klaxon sounded, and Katherine snapped her head to stare at the Command console. A red "Alert-First Priority" flashed on all visible screens around her and, no doubt, on dozens more.

Lori leaned over and tapped the screen closest to her. "A personal emergency signal has been activated by a senior officer. I can't tell whose it is. O'Connor?"

The young communications officer stared at his screen, fingers flying across it, as he tapped several touch buttons over and over. Finally, he grunted and looked around. "Well, there are four senior officers in OPs. I'll guess it's not one of you."

Katherine cocked an eyebrow and asked, "Why isn't the computer recognizing the signals?"

Williams answered. "Upgrading the internal systems was on the low priority list, so those greenhorns probably pulled down the sensor protocols as well."

Katherine nodded. She looked over at a young, plump woman. "All right. Ensign Delyth?"

"Yes, Captain?"

"Signal every senior officer not in OPs and see who doesn't respond."

"Yes, Captain."

Katherine turned back to O'Connor. "Put security on alert. Have them check the cargo bays and any low-traffic areas for suspicious activity."

Adrenaline pumped into her blood stream and the aches of her injures blurred a little. Her thoughts focused on the emergency signal.

O'Connor looked at her, his eyes wide. "It would take a week at least to search the entire port."

"Then let's get started," she snapped. Pre-war, she would have never allowed ensigns to work in OPs. These days, there wasn't much choice. All the more reason for her to stay focused on the task—bringing the Alliance into the war.

"Yes, Captain!" O'Connor responded and busied himself. He shouted orders to the cadet stationed next to him. Katherine did not interfere.

"Captain, I... This can't be right," Windrunner said, her gaze going between Katherine and the console.

Katherine leaned forward. "What is it?"

"According to scans, Randall White is on board."

Katherine licked her lips, and her heart sank. Several lies flooded her mind in the following seconds, as she tried to find the best way to avoid raising too many suspicions. She had not anticipated an emergency that caused a port-wide scan. She should have thought of that, should have put up a dampening field in the area.

"Captain, apparently he's in Cargo Bay Eleven."

Katherine blinked. That wasn't anywhere near the Ambassador suites. "Are you certain?"

Windrunner stepped aside, so that Katherine could look

at the console. True enough, White's life-sign scan blinked in Cargo Bay Eleven. "MacDonald, what's in that bay?"

The older man didn't need to consult his console. "Parts headed for reclamation. Lieutenant Raewadee has been working in that area most of the day."

Katherine swore under her breath. She had put one of Perditions' youngest officers in mortal danger. "O'Connor, full security alert, critical priority. Do not alert the general population. I don't want White to know we're looking for him."

Though her joints ached, and a mounting headache pounded, Katherine stepped to the weapons locker on the wall closest to the Command area. She keyed in the pass-code and paused for a retinal scan. The magnetic lock thumped, and the door popped open a centimeter, enough for her to slip her fingers behind. She flung the door open, grabbed a pulse rifle and tossed it to a confused Lori. She grabbed a smaller stun pistol for herself.

"Langtry, Austen, fall in with us," Katherine said, handing out weapons. She turned to O'Connor and said, "I'm leaving you in charge of communications. Keep us up to date, Ensign. I'll need you on your best game."

The red-head stared at her, wide-eyed, but gave a stiff nod of his head. Considering she no longer had a chief of communications, O'Connor was sadly the most qualified.

"Commander Williams, I'm leaving you in charge of OPs. Cho, you're in charge of coordinating the rescue mission from here with Commander Ambrose and myself. We are working with the assumption that Lieutenant Raewadee is in danger, and Randall White is somehow involved until you can show otherwise."

"Um, Captain, what are you doing?" Windrunner asked, low enough that no one else would hear.

Katherine ignored her. Instead, she flipped the metal switch on her weapon, and it hummed to life. The energy bar registered at full power. "MacDonald, send a heavily-armed team and a medic to the Ambassador wing. They are not to arrest anyone in that area unless it's White himself."

"Doing it now, Captain."

"What is going on?" Windrunner growled, her voice a little louder.

"We need to get going. There's a lot of territory down there to cover."

"You can barely stand."

Katherine shot her the sternest look she could muster. "Right now, we're down nearly forty security guards while we wait for Fleet to send us more. Perdition is a big port, and we know it better than anyone else in OPs right now. The more time we stand here talking, the more time Randall White has to rape and murder his way through the docking port.

"Let's go," Katherine said, not waiting for a reply. She grimaced against the mounting pain as she worried about Bindu, Salim, and the guards in his wing. Had he killed Salim, Prasad, and the other guards? Had he attacked Bindu, and she called for help, not realizing that the sensors were off-line? Had White escaped on a ship?

Rage mounted in Katherine. She'd brought this murderer onto Perdition. She'd take him down.

CHAPTER NINETEEN

Despite the aches in her joints and the stinging in her muscles, Katherine pushed through the pain and kept a fast pace to the cargo area. She could take a double dose of meds later and knock herself into a coma. Right now, she had to find a murderer.

"Captain!"

"Ambrose, report."

Ambrose came to a stop, while her team fanned out in different directions. "I have most of Perdition's security force spread out through the cargo areas, plus a tier up and down. I've called in reinforcements from docked ships to help secure key facilities and to enforce the lockdown, especially with people trying to get out of the habitat areas."

Katherine nodded. "Good. Any word from the Ambassador wing yet?"

Nova shook her head, concern etched on her weathered features.

Katherine tapped her earpiece. "O'Connor, any word from the teams in the Ambassador quarters?"

"No, we haven't heard anything from that section yet. Wait. Sorry, sir?" His voice died off, clearly speaking to someone in a console near him. "Commander Williams said there is a fire in the Ambassador wing, and reinforcements were called in. He'll update you as soon as he has more."

"Ambrose here," Nova said, touching her own ear piece. "Divert Kiyawasew's team toward the wing. He should be the closest." She paused. "Hold. Captain, do you have O'Connor on the line?" Katherine asked, "O'Connor, can you still hear me?"

"Yes, Captain."

"O'Connor, I've put you on open speaker. Ambrose, go ahead."

"Who is the closest team to Dock Eleven?"

Beeps and the background flurry of officers at work went on before O'Connor answered. "Ensign Douglass."

"Someone else?" Ambrose frowned and whispered to Katherine, "He's been on Perdition half a day. Probably doesn't even know where Dock Eleven is."

"Master Corporal Wynne is at Dock Ten."

"Have her team break. Half stays in place, the other heads over to Eleven to cover. Ambrose out."

"Francis out."

Katherine licked her lips. She hoped that Salim, Prasad, and the other guards were uninjured. Obviously, she was worried for Bindu, too. But, mostly, she was furious at herself. If anything happened to any of them, she would never forgive herself. White was there to bring about peace, not add violence to Perdition. They didn't need his help for that; the Coalition gave them enough trouble.

"Let's all fan out. We have a lot of bays to cover," Katherine said. Ambrose nodded and caught up with her group that was broken between two bays about fifty meters ahead. Then, Katherine turned to Lori and said, "Let's take Bay Three."

The storage bay was silent. Quiet was normal; silent was not. The overhead lights sluggishly hummed to life when they walked through. Katherine, Lori, and the two junior ranks she pulled from OPs stepped into the large, cluttered room and looked around, weapons at the ready.

Lori nudged her and pointed. At the furthest end of the bay, a jungle of conveyor belts sat motionless. So too was the robotic arm that normally deposited the scrap metal on the belts to be sent to reclamation. The bay was a metal forest, compressed quarter meter cubes of different materials. She looked around at the precious metals storage. Bundles of platinum, silver, and gold pieces were pressed together. Metal bins lined one wall with labels of "diamond shards," "gold pieces," and "titanium pieces," and other cargo bins held small pieces of miscellaneous refuse, too small to bundle yet large enough to reprocess into something useful. No one could hide within the bundles of metals, wires, and plastics.

They made their way slowly through the man-made walkways to maneuver around the room. Katherine looked up as often as around... White could be on top of a metal stack with a stun grenade. Or, a pulse charge.

"Something isn't right here," Katherine mumbled. "Why are the belts off?"

"I agree, Captain. Something isn't right here," Lori said, her tone matching Katherine's. She took an additional step to stand next to Katherine. She glanced over her shoulder before saying, in a lowered voice, "For one thing, you weren't surprised that Randall White was on the station."

"No, I wasn't." Katherine swallowed as they stepped through the littered pathways. She had known this conversation would eventually happen. She wished it hadn't been now. "He was supposed to be here for a few days and then returned to Arcon Penal Colony."

"You haven't said why."

Katherine stopped walking. "Intel."

It was the only truth of the situation she could dredge up. Lying did not come naturally to her. Rumor had it that Intel offered a lying course for third-year operatives studying surveillance gathering. She could've used that course. A small voice said it wasn't too late.

Lori cocked an eyebrow, her usual look of disbelief. "And this Intel work couldn't happen at Arcon?"

Katherine shook her head, and they started walking again, this time closer to the belts, where they led to the next bay for sorting. "No. He was never supposed to get out. I had guards posted—"

"Where the hell did you get the guards without me knowing about the duty reassignment?"

"Welcome to being second-in-command and learning how little you know about port-side politics," she said, not bothering to smile. "Let's discuss this later. Right now, let's try to find this asshole."

Lori nodded, and the two women headed further into the bay. They had gone through the entire area. Nothing. Katherine shook her head. "There's no one here."

Lori asked, "How can you be sure? Someone turned off all the belts. It's a perfect place to hide in here."

Katherine shook her head. "Randall White didn't escape to hide away. He escaped to hurt people."

"News Net used to say he was cured. I remember a lot of stories on it. That's what prompted the Union ban on all neural interfaces until further study was completed. Maybe he simply wants off the station so that he doesn't have to go back to the colony."

Katherine pondered that. "You know, I don't think he'd be in here. He's former Intel. Hiding doesn't seem his style. Staying a few steps ahead of us does." She tapped her ear piece. "Francis to O'Connor."

"Hi again, Captain."

Katherine sighed. She had no one else to blame but herself. O'Connor studied engineering at UFU, but John had reassigned him to Communications. They had enough barely trained engineers and not nearly enough people who could operate a comm console. Some...roughness was to be expected. "Report."

O'Connor um'ed and ah'ed before answering. "Lieutenant Raewadee is the only officer who hasn't reported in. I sent a team to her quarters, but she wasn't there. I also sent a team to Harold Anderson's quarters, but she wasn't there, either."

"The barber? Why him?"

He cleared his throat and said, in a low voice, "Ah, they're... friendly."

Katherine's eyes widened. "Oh. Let's go on full alert. Put out the rumor. Get out that it's a training exercise. Only Security Level Ten are to be aware of what they are looking for."

"What should I tell our people?"

Katherine frowned, even if O'Connor couldn't see it. "Tell them I am displeased with the complete lack of independent thought amongst the junior ranks, so I've staged a prisoner escape. To make things more interesting, I've deployed a man with image distorters to make him look like the Union's greatest criminal. Now, they have to avoid causing a major panic amongst the civilians."

"Yes, Captain." She could almost see the blush on his cheeks. O'Connor was a good enough kid, even if he did lack the necessary skills to be working OPs communications in a busy space port. But it was either him or pull a qualified person out of the command structure. She couldn't afford that with their manpower shortage. She'd have to find the time to get him trained up. There was no one else.

Katherine looked around the room. She opened a line with Williams and ordered, "Erect a security gate around this entire section, five levels up and down. Send in all the sweep drones to assist. I want the entire duct system swept, too. On foot, White couldn't have gone far. Lock down all ships in dock and have them search their vessels. All ships to have left in the last three hours are ordered to remain where they are and search for a prisoner. They're still in our space, so they have to comply."

"Yes, Captain."

"Francis out."

Katherine motioned to the small opening where the belt went into the processing room. She crawled in through the small hole, wincing as she pulled herself through. Sharp, eye-watering pain cut through the side of her neck, and Katherine rolled on her back, still on the belt, clasping her muscles in her hand. While she held her back tight, trying to massage the spasm into submission, she noticed a red smear on top of the fabricator.

A partial, but recognizable, bloody hand print.

She traced upwards and found another smear on the ceiling. She looked to the floor and saw a small dusting of tile powder. Someone had pulled out a ceiling tile and accessed the upper vent system.

Katherine tapped her ear piece and whispered, "Francis to O'Connor."

"Yes, Captain?"

"Shut down all the vents in this area. Get ready to pump gas into them."

"Um, what kind of gas?"

"Just tell Commander Williams what I said," she snapped, trying to keep her voice at a whisper. How could he not know they had installed anesthetizing gas throughout the duct system, after the first attack on Perdition when they'd been boarded? She shook her head.

"What's going on?" Windrunner asked, sticking her head through the hole.

Katherine held her finger to her lips and pointed up. In a normal voice, she said, "Hurt my neck climbing through here. I'll be fine. Let's do a quick look and move on. I think he's moved to the next level already. I've asked O'Connor to raise the security fields while we get everyone into place to storm Level Forty-one."

Lori stared at the bloody print on the ceiling and nodded. "Sounds good."

They motioned for the two junior officers to come through, giving them the silent cue as well. Lori touched her ear piece and whispered for Ambrose to get her people into place. Katherine led them into the next room, unhooked the engineering ladder from the wall and motioned for Lori, Landry, and Austen to climb up and into the ceiling shafts.

Katherine carried up in the rear. She would have normally gone first, but with her injuries, she knew she could not move fast enough in case of a chase. The initial crawl space was just that, a claustrophobic dungeon. However, it transitioned into a more manageable standing area, though only wide enough to pull off a work panel to fix pipes, wiring, or power. The *whoosh* of the horizontal lift went by every few seconds, as it glided along magnetic tracks. There was enough noise for her to doubt White could have heard her in the previous room.

However, further down the hall, hidden from view, Katherine heard the distinctive muffled "bitch," followed by a thud and a stream of swearing.

From a female.

Lori must have heard it, too, because she quickened her step. Katherine limped along, keeping pace as she fought the rising pain. She had a suppressor shot in her pocket, but she didn't want to use it. It made her rather euphoric; she needed her wits alive and raw, not dull and dazed. The adrenaline pumping through her was more than enough to maintain her for a few moments.

Lori turned the corner first, the corridor echoed with the *whump* of the back-blast from her stun rifle. Katherine pulled in front of Lori. The small alcove housed the electrical controls for the level's lift. White was little more than a tangled lump of limbs. Lori's stun rifle would only keep him out for seconds, a minute at most, but the after effects would linger for an hour: enough time to get him into a secure holding area.

Katherine heard a muffled whimper and saw Bindu suspended from the ceiling. One side of her face was melted off, ragged pink meat hanging where her smooth, brown skin once was. Her lovely, youthful features were replaced with bruises, swelling, and that vicious burn on her cheek. The acrid air singed Katherine's nose hair, and her eyes watered.

Fury rushed through Katherine. Her hands shook as adrenaline pumped through her veins. Ensign Langtry was the tallest and able to reach Bindu's hands, bound and hanging from where a light once dangled.

The young engineer crumpled to the ground, even though Langtry tried to ease her down. Katherine stared at the ragged officer and the slowly awakening Randall White.

Rapist. Assassin. Genius.

Butcher.

Chills gripped her.

"Butcher," she whispered, staring at him.

"Captain?" Windrunner asked, narrowing her eyes. "Austen, if he flinches, shoot him." She went to tap her ear piece, but Katherine grabbed her arm.

"Take the kids into the hall," Katherine growled. She let go and flipped the safety off on her projectile rifle. The pulse chamber hummed. She steadied her stance.

Windrunner looked between Katherine and White, who slowly stirred, moaning.

Katherine did not move. "Do as I ordered."

"It's murder if you do it, Katherine," Windrunner whispered.

"I need to talk to him, Commander. Alone."

Letting White live meant she'd have to deal with the mess of an investigation, arrest, trial, and dragging her entire plan into the open. A corpse, however, could not defend itself. A corpse of the most hated man in the Fleet would not get the same attention as a living perpetrator.

"All right." Windrunner sighed but ordered Ensigns Langtry and Austen to carry Bindu out, so she could stay with White and Katherine. "I'm not leaving."

"Lori, if you interfere—"

Windrunner turned her back on White and Katherine. She crossed her arms. "Bastard hurt Bindu. He can rot in hell, for all I care. I'm sticking around to make sure you have an alibi."

Katherine would have smiled, but there was nothing to smile about. She was about to kill a man and felt no remorse.

Katherine counted to fifteen before tapping her ear piece. She took a deep breath and said, "O'Connor, I have White on Level Forty, in the lift's repair lines. Send a full medical team. Lieutenant Raewadee has been severely injured. White's been stunned and..." Katherine swallowed and let out a curse. She slammed her rifle against the wall twice and mumbled incoherently.

"Captain? Captain, are you all right?" O'Connor's voice went shrill. "Captain, answer me!"

Then, Katherine raised her weapon, slowly, deliberately and shot Randall White in the face.

At least, she aimed to do that. With unsteady arms caused by pain and adrenaline, she shot him in the upper chest. Blood bubbled through his clothes, slowly making its way down his limp body.

"Captain! Commander Williams, shots fired! Shots fired! I think White shot the Captain."

Katherine ignored the open communications line and stared at the dying body of White. She felt the last shred of her own morality bleed out with him and spread in a puddle around her. She'd never be able to put it back. She'd killed in cold blood. It wasn't to protect the innocently young Second Lieutenant Bindu Raewadee. It was to protect her career. White stirred enough to give her a knowing smile.

She'd turned into him.

CHAPTER TWENTY

Katherine stared at her reflection in the mirror. She didn't recognize the person staring back. Her eyes were bloodshot and sunken from too little sleep and too much stress. Her hair drooped over her face, hanging limply. Her normally fair skin now had a pallid hue to it. Stress acne broke out on her chin.

She'd received a coded message from Patricia. She'd be arriving within three days. Her ship was probably dodging Coalition patrols at this very minute. Why that woman decided to work at a civilian hospital in spitting distance from the front she'd never understand.

Of course, that's why Patricia left her. Because she didn't understand. Oh, Katherine pretended to be smart and clever, but Patricia had been right all along. She was a monster. She killed Randall White, in a cold, calculating murder.

The most damning part of it all? She'd do it again.

And again.

And fucking again.

She'd keep doing it if it meant she could bring the Alliance into the war and end the bloodshed. The truth sickened her.

Mechanically, Katherine screwed the top off the medication jar and set it aside. She dipped her fingers into the cream and rubbed it on her broken-out chin. All the while, she forced herself to peer into the reflection of her own eyes. She'd condemned this young woman, once full of life and vibrancy, to a life of fear, mistrust, and paranoia. All in the sacred name of peace.

Yes, she would look herself in the mirror. And she would hate what stared back because it was all she deserved now.

"Incoming message from Salim Tobin," the intercom chirped.

"Computer, voice only." A ping announced the transfer was successful. "Good morning, Salim."

"Good morning, Captain. I want to advise you that—"

"Is the meeting still on?" Katherine snapped.

"Yes," Salim drawled out.

"Then that's all I care about. Cut to the details once we are off the station."

She could almost hear Salim blink in the silent moment that followed. "Of course, Captain. I will see you at Landing Pad Forty-five as planned."

The connection pinged and ended. She went back to grooming, combing her shoulder length hair. Once done, she secured it into a pony tail at the nape of her neck.

She tapped the panel again and put in a call to Lori. Katherine was pulling on the trousers of her uniform when Lori answered.

"Is everything set for my departure?"

"Yes, Captain," the voice said from the other line. "I'll look after things while you are gone. Do you know how long your mission will last?"

"Should only be a couple of days. However, if I'm not back within four, I've instructed the computer to send you additional instructions."

Lori hesitated for a moment. There was a click, and Katherine was aware Lori had transferred the call to her ear piece. In a whisper, Lori asked, "Is everything all right?"

Katherine pulled her tunic on and began buttoning it up. She kept her tone steady and even, though her insides flopped around. "Yes. I have a classified mission. You know how it is."

"Is there anything I can do to help?"

Katherine wondered if Lori meant about the mission or

about White's death. *Murder*, she corrected herself. Murder. "Keep Landing Pad Forty-five cleared as best you can, so that I can slip out without being noticed. I'd prefer if my helper wasn't identified during the process."

"Already done. You're safe."

Katherine was about to sign off, but she asked, "How is Bindu?"

Lori swallowed. "She's been pushing for a full investigation about why White was on the station. I asked her to consider dropping it, but that made her angry. She's insisting to speak with you."

Katherine clucked her tongue against the roof of her mouth. Visiting Bindu in the hospital was at the bottom of things she wanted to do. How could she tell the young officer to stop pursuing White's death?

Lori cleared her throat. "Um, Ambrose stamped our statements about White's death. She'd close the file as self-defense, but Raewadee won't let her."

Katherine swallowed.She flipped her gaze at the digital clock. She had an hour. That allowed enough time to get to the hospital, spend five awkward moments, and then make it to the docking ring. "All right. I'll make a quick stop. Keep the landing pad clear until I've launched."

"Good hunting." Lori's line went dead.

Katherine took a steadying, deep breath. She could look herself in the mirror. Surely, she could look into the eyes of the woman she helped assault.

The walk to the hospital was uneventful. The initial euphoria of her medication had subsided, so she could remain somber and upright at the same time. The closer she got to the hospital, however, the tighter her stomach clenched.

A dark-skinned swollen mess lay limp on the hospital bed. Half of her hair was missing, replaced with sterile white bandages. Monitors on the wall displayed various graphs, moving up and down in a steady rhythm. They meant nothing to Katherine, but the consistency was probably a good sign.

The lump of flesh moved, revealing a swollen, disfigured woman. Katherine swallowed and cleared her throat. Shimmering film covered one side of Bindu's face. Dr. Kramer was confident that, after three reconstructive surgeries, her face would resemble its old self. For now, they had to focus on regenerating the strips of flesh that had been burned off.

"I'm sorry to disturb you. I'll be leaving for a few days and wanted to talk to you," Katherine said, keeping her tone even.

Bindu nodded. She licked her blistered, swollen lips and winced. "Thanks for coming."

"How are you feeling?" Katherine's breakfast churned.

She gave a weak shrug. "Doc says I will be here for a while yet. They're still afraid of infection."

Katherine nodded but remained quiet. She needed to bring up the investigation but couldn't find the words. How could she ask this girl, and Bindu was a girl in Katherine's eyes, to give up her search for answers? How could she take away that closure from her?

Katherine took a deep breath, knowing she'd hate herself forever for what was about to come out of her mouth. "Bindu, I need to ask a favor."

"Of course, *Katherine*," the young woman said, her once rich voice now ragged and dry.

Oh God. Katherine gulped. She'd never called her that before outside of the Sunday suppers. Katherine had earned Bindu's complete trust, and she was about to trample it. Katherine forced the words out, her voice husky and somber. "I need you to let the investigation close."

"What?"

"Do it."

Katherine could see the last shreds of Bindu's spirit crushed in her eyes, but she stared at the brown, watery orbs. She took a long, slow breath. It had been a mistake to let herself grow fond of the girl. It was war, and she could not afford any closeness or new friends in lower ranks under her command. Not now when they fought for their very survival.

"You brought him. He came because of you," she whispered, choking back tears.

"Lieutenant Raewadee, drop the investigation."

Raewadee looked away for several moments before saying, "What happens if I don't?"

"I—" Katherine's voice cracked and she cleared her throat. "I will order Ambrose to close the investigation after I detail how you wasted security resource time on a closed case and order you to undergo a psych evaluation."

Raewadee's mouth hung open, an audible gasp coming from her. Chills spread through Katherine, but she clenched her muscles and did not shake.

"Why?" Raewadee did not hide her tears now. She motioned at her bandaged face. "Look at me. Why wouldn't you want me to find some peace?"

Katherine twitched but held her ground. "Lieutenant, I have nothing but sympathy for your situation—"

"Fuck your sympathy," she snarled. "Fuck you. You did this to me."

Hatred welled up inside Katherine. She stepped up to Raewadee and slammed her hands on the hospital bed, glaring down at the young woman, who had to lean back to avoid butting heads. "Listen to me because I will only ever let you get away with speaking like that this one time. I know I did this to you. I would do it again. Do you understand me? Your comfort, your looks, your vanity mean nothing to me right now. If you aren't willing to give up something as simple as your pretty little face, then get the hell off my station."

Regret immediately slammed against Katherine, but too much fury raced through her veins for her to care. She spun on her heel to exit the room. She did stop at the door, unable to leave without offering some apology. "If you want a transfer, name it. Any position, military or civilian. Name it, and I'll get you it. But if you want to stay on Perdition, you will drop the investigation."

With that, Katherine left and headed toward Landing Pad 45. There was no time for regrets. Later, she could drown them in John's single malt collection to her heart's content.

CHAPTER TWENTY-ONE

The abandoned mining complex on New Titan had seen better days. Corrosive rain that fell for several hours a day had begun to pit its metallic structure. Despite having one of the richest deposits of deuterium in the sector, the mine ended operations after only six years. The natural corrosive rain made it impossible to properly maintain the equipment. More time was spent on repairs than actual drilling.

Katherine expertly guided the tiny shuttle into the small opening at one of the exterior landing pads. The ship let out a hiss as it settled on the ground.

"Excellent landing, Captain," Salim said in his usual jovial tone.

Katherine didn't answer. The proverbial bad feeling spread through her. Her instincts told her things were about to skid sideways and in such a graphic and spectacular fashion that history books would recount the day's events for centuries to come.

Of course, she dismissed the thought as quickly as it formed. Melodramatic nonsense had no place in her brain and definitely not on a mission. She was in chest-deep; she knew it. There was only one legal way to extract herself, and she wasn't ready to issue the surrender order on her career. Not yet.

Katherine looked over her shoulder at the four black-clad guards, the ones who had guarded White. They'd more or less recovered from their injuries. Prasad sported a brace on each wrist, while the others kept their bruises hidden by their tinted visors. A purple-hued welt covered the majority of Salim's right cheek and jawline.

"Stay here," she said to the guards. It wasn't an ideal situation, but at least they were already trustworthy. From their spotty and heavily-censored records, they had been on enough Intel missions to know to keep their mouths shut.

Still, the fewer people who knew what she was doing, the better. If the guards stayed in the shuttle, they wouldn't find out anything of importance. At worst, they'd notice a commercial ship landing, in which Junior Delegate Arthur Frum was supposedly arriving.

Katherine pressed the panel and waited for the door to slide open. A six-foot ramp slid from a hidden compartment, and she stepped down it into the heart of the sheltered landing area. Salim stepped out behind her, but they didn't linger. Rain splashed only a few feet from them. Even in her protective gear, Katherine hurried to get inside.

"Why are you following me, Salim?"

"Captain, I told my good friend, Arthur, that I would introduce you to him. He wanted assurances that you were not here to kill him, or some such." Salim waved a dismissive hand.

Katherine wheeled around. "Why in God's name would I kill him? I want the Alliance on our side. I'm not here to assassinate him."

Salim took a deep breath before shrugging. "He's rather irrational."

"Indeed. I am, as well, when it comes to you, Salim Tobin. I like to keep you where I can see you. Otherwise, you could be playing a game on the side."

Katherine turned toward the voice. A man stepped out from the shadows of an unlit corridor. He was a short man, his white teeth gleamed against his tanned skin and pink gums. He dressed casually, more like a merchant or a civilian, than an official dignitary. However, considering the shadiness of the entire meeting, perhaps it wasn't such a bad idea.

Once they both closed the distance, Salim said, "Arthur, allow me the pleasure to introduce Captain Katherine Francis. Captain, this is my old friend, Junior Delegate Arthur Frum."

Frum snorted.

"Thank you for meeting with me." Katherine offered a polite smile and extended her hand. He shook it and gave her a smile.

"Oh, please. Do not thank me. I've been indebted to... *Salim*, is it now...for long enough. I was happy to settle the balance sheet."

That raised the hairs on Katherine's neck. Intel had various supposed aliases for him but nothing concrete. She watched the two men glare at each other, hate in Frum's eyes and amusement in Salim's.

"Captain, now we are acquainted, and you have come unarmed and unguarded, I'd like to speak with you alone."

Katherine glanced at Salim and back at the well-armed guards further down the hallway.

"He can enjoy the protection of my guards."

"If you wish, Salim can return to our ship. I have brought Union soldiers with me, and they can ensure Salim's *protection*."

Frum let out a frustrated sigh and shook his head. "I trust the reputation of your Fleet's soldiers as hardy, loyal people. Sadly, however, I would not trust Salim to stir my morning coffee. My terms are non-negotiable."

"Don't worry, Captain. I'll stand right here and admire these fine soldiers. It's been several years since I've had the pleasure to be in the presence of such greatness."

She resisted an eye roll. Frum, however, did not, and Katherine gave him a half smirk of approval. Frum motioned ahead, and they walked down the only lit corridor option. When further out of hearing, she said, "There is a history between the two of you?"

The delegate laughed. "What did Salim tell you?"

"That he rescued your sister, and you will carry out any

reasonable request to help repay the kindness."

"You jest."

Katherine stared at him blankly. Even though she felt like the only person not in on some kind of practical joke, she tried her utmost to hide it. Silence was often the key to maintaining a façade and aura of mystery.

Frum shook his head. "No, I suppose you do not."

"He repeatedly said that he rescued your sister. With Salim, he rarely repeats the same thing twice."

Frum laughed again. "Yes, of course he'd say that. What he failed to tell you is how she ended up needing rescue and how Salim blackmailed me in the process."

There might have been a time when Katherine would have been shocked by the statement. Not any longer. Working with Salim taught her one thing: his file didn't do him justice. Instead, she smiled. "Salim's ability to tell half-truths is indeed a rare gift."

He laughed. "Yes, it is. So, Captain Katherine Francis of the Docking Port Perdition, why am I here on this abandoned rock?"

Katherine's stomach tightened, but she kept her breath steady. "Salim didn't tell you?"

"Oh, he said something about vital information regarding the security of Alliance territory. Coming from Salim, however, one tends to question the entire transmission."

Katherine struggled to hold back the shakes. She hoped he would dismiss it as part of her physical condition, not her emotional state. "Union Intel obtained some files of note."

He raised his eyebrows. "Go on."

"They contain the Coalition's infiltration of the Alliance military and government."

He stared at her before breaking into choking laughter. Katherine stared at him, uncertain if he was laughing or choking on his own tongue. He turned red-faced as he was buckled over, slapping his thigh.

Katherine furrowed her brow. "I don't understand what

is so funny."

He eased up the laughter, still gasping for breath. "Oh Captain, that was glorious. Thank you. Now, seriously, what did they find?"

She thought of John, her sister, her step-mother, and everyone she'd ever known killed by the Coalition's war. She even though of Raewadee, wrapped in translucent healing gauze. The poker face held, even hardened. "Successful infiltration."

He licked his lips, staring at her. "You expect me to believe that your intelligence people have broken into Coalition headquarters and obtained mythical documents exposing the Coalition's treachery. And, from the kindness of your heart and your innate good will, you are giving this information to me?"

Katherine did not move. She kept her body as rigid as possible, terrified that moving would be seen as a flinch. "It isn't in good will."

He cocked an eyebrow.

"I want the Alliance to enter the war."

He stared, wide-eyed, before nodding, a slow, methodical motion of his head. "Yes, now that I believe. All right. Let me see this Holy Grail of documentation."

Katherine handed him an official-looking faux wood box. It was actually plastic, but the sheen and texture was a decent replica. On the top was the Union's emblem and flag.

He opened it, never taking his eyes off her. She did notice that he flipped the box open toward her, not toward himself. One corner of her mouth went up over his mistrust. She'd have to remember that particular slight for any future dicey situations. Then again, she prayed that this would be her first and last mission for Intel or Black OPs, or whatever the hell they called what she was doing.

Treason.

She pushed the word out of her mind as fast as it arrived. Thinking that particular thought would have her sweating and shaking within moments, and her limited Intel skills said that would be a bad thing. So, she stood there, statuesque as much as humanly possible.

"I'll need to take this back to my ship to examine it."

"Of course," Katherine said, keeping her tone neutral.

He stared at her, hard. "If this is a fake, I will rain down destruction on your people in a manner that will make you wish the Coalition conquered you, do you understand?"

Katherine resisted the gulp, as she resisted leaning back away from him. She stared at him, as blankly as she could, thinking benign thoughts, like the current discussion over whether all fleet officers should have communications implants installed in their cerebral cortex.

"And if it is true?"

He turned to her, a faint smile on his face. "You will get to enjoy victory over your enemies."

With that, he walked down the hallway, until he met up with his guards. When they turned the corner, Katherine let out her breath and felt her muscles unclench. The world turned on end for a moment, the adrenaline surging through her as the moment of bluff passed. She had pulled it off. She had lied to someone square in the face.

Now, the true test would be if all the work, all the sacrifice had been worth it.

CHAPTER TWENTY-TWO

Katherine headed back to the ship, since the investigation of the data chips would take at least an hour. She paced as much as possible while using a cane. She poured herself a cup of coffee, which she didn't drink. She got herself a bran muffin, which she left...somewhere.

Thoughts and images and the worries of failure nagged at her, threatening to rip apart her sanity. So much rode on her ability to pull off this meeting: White's forgery, Frum, everything. There was no turning back, no time to second guess or question herself. Either she'd succeed and the Alliance would enter the war, or she'd spend her life at a maximum security penal colony, where no one would visit her ever. Not even Patricia.

The mere thought of her wife's name tugged at the edges of her nerves, and she pushed the thoughts and memories aside. Time to fret and collapse later. Right now, it was time to wait and be calm.

She looked at the guards. They sat quietly, occasionally talking to each other. A massive guard appeared to be sleeping, his head tipped to one side on the chair. But, mostly, they were silent. They were on a mission and chatter had no place.

Then, she noticed someone was missing. "Where is Salim?"

The man she thought was asleep answered in a voice that sounded too young to possess such bulk. "Back storage. He said to leave him be."

Katherine frowned and immediately went to the back area of the shuttle. Leaving him to do what he wanted was never a good plan. She opened the door, not bothering with the chime. No point in signaling her approach. The door slid open, and Katherine found Salim on the carpeted floor with a data pad, reading.

She had expected him to jump or struggle to hide something. He didn't. In fact, he appeared completely at ease. That made her even more suspicious. "What are you doing?"

He raised his eyebrows at her tone. "Reading. I take it we're at the inspection stage of the negotiations."

Katherine nodded, annoyed that he'd misdirected the conversation. Damn, he was good.

"What are your plans if he determines they are fakes?"

Katherine gulped. "I have no plans."

Salim stared at her, his eyes wide. "Captain, you have no backup plan?"

Katherine showed him her palms. "I assumed that after his guards tackled me and put me into shackles, I'd be paraded on every computer screen from here to hell."

Salim thought on that before he said, "Ah, you do have a Plan B. Outstanding."

Katherine gave him a level look. "Don't play with me, Salim. What is it that you're doing?"

He glanced at his pad. "I doubt you want to know, but if you insist, I'm investigating our Mr. Frum's financial records. Did you know he had four million credits transferred to his account only an hour ago?"

"He did?" Katherine blinked. "Wait, you gave him money?"

Salim shook his head. "No, no, it wasn't from me. If I had several million credits, the last thing I'd do is give them to the likes of him. No, indeed, someone has transferred him money. I wonder why. I should go ask him."

Katherine cocked an eyebrow, a little dread filling her. "Do you think he's told anyone about our meeting?"

Salim shrugged, but before he could speak, Katherine added, "No. Wait. He's been paid because he's agreed to do something for the Coalition. They've bribed him."

Salim smiled. "That sounds like the Arthur Frum I know. Weasels are always the easiest to detect worming their way through life."

Katherine's eyes grew wide. "But, that means he'll expose us."

"Yup."

"Salim! He's going to discover those documents are a fake. He might even say they are because he's being bribed to do something else."

"There's no sense worrying about it." Salim went back to reading his data pad.

Katherine put her hands on her hips. "Easy for you to say. You aren't going to spend the rest of your life in prison for treason."

"My dear Captain, if they discover that it's all faked, we won't have to worry about prison."

"No?"

"No. We'll be dead."

Katherine gulped at that.

The comm system buzzed, and Frum's voice spoke. "Captain Francis, would you come outside please?"

Katherine did not like the tone. She fiddled with her side arm. It was still there. She nodded at her guards, who flipped their safety catches off. Then, she stepped out of the ship. At least it had stopped raining.

Frum was surrounded by six guards. His face was red, angry. Her stomach dropped. Frum threw a data pad on the muddy ground.

"It is a fake."

CHAPTER TWENTY-THREE

Events unfolded at such a pace that, if questioned later, Katherine would not have been able to put it all in order. She remembered the box containing the counterfeit data pads smashing to the ground, though she could not confirm if that was before or after an energy beam strafed centimeters in front of her face.

Katherine dove underneath the extended landing supports of her shuttle. The mud and her protective suit carried her further than she'd planned to go, and she slammed her head against one of the exhaust vents. The world danced for a moment. With only two feet of room between the underbelly and the sinking pit of mud, she was a hard target to hit. Unfortunately, it also made it difficult for her to readjust herself to aim at any target of her own.

She opened fire with her energy weapon on stun. Prasad slid under the ship alongside her, splashing corrosive water and mud all over her face, about the only part of her not covered with protector gear. They'd all need an hour in decon after this.

Fleet guards dove for cover near their shuttle. The delegate's security force likewise retreated toward their shuttle. Bullets and beams littered the no man's land in between.

Katherine aimed and fired. Her shot hit Frum's shoulder, threw him off balance, and he crashed against the side of the

Alliance ship, before collapsing to the ground. Blood seeped from his head.

"Captain, get inside!" Prasad shouted over the thunder of his own weapon. A spread of projectile bullets littered the air. Katherine clenched her eyelids shut and waited for the lightshow to subside.

"I don't remember giving you a micro explosives launcher," she quipped, not breaking from shooting. Then she shouted loud enough for her own people to hear her, "Inside the shuttle! Now!"

"Captain..."

"Shut up. I'm providing suppression fire."

A string of bullets assaulted the shuttle's underbelly. Metal and bullet casings smacked Katherine's body. Between the pain-suppressors and the rush of battle, she didn't feel more than the slight annoyance of its pressing weight.

"Salim! Help me!" Prasad shouted. Katherine did not stop firing her stun weapon.

Everyone screamed around her. Curses, oaths, and the chaotic shouting of orders rang through the air. Katherine ignored it all. Instead, she turned her attention to Frum's unconscious body and flipped her rifle setting from "stun" to "blast." She aimed and squeezed.

Katherine couldn't say whether it was her weapon that took him out. A spray of projectiles bounced off the ground around him and littered the limp, chewed meat that was once his body.

Her heart pounded as adrenaline again pumped through her veins. In a few moments, she knew the pain of moving too much would overtake her, and she'd be near disabled.

Frum's ship started firing at them.

Salim grabbed Katherine's forearms and dragged her from under the ship, while Prasad maintained the thunder and lightning show. Stars twinkled in Katherine's eyes from the brilliance of the explosives.

"Get inside! Now! Everyone inside! Captain, unlock the control," Prasad shouted.

Salim and Prasad helped her into the shuttle. Her legs wobbled, and her shoulder blades ached from where a large piece of metal hit her earlier. Katherine estimated she had about two minutes before the adrenaline rush faded and the brain-numbing pain arrived. At least, the meds helped some.

Katherine entered the shuttle and immediately shouted, before even taking a seat, "Computer, unlock console, authorization code Delta-Echo-Charlie-Eighteen."

"December eighteenth." Salim looked at her, bemused. "Your wedding date?"

"It isn't meant to be a high security password." Katherine scowled and strapped herself into her chair. She winced, trying to pull the second brace over her left arm. One of the guards lifted it into place for her. "It's to prevent someone from leaning on the console and firing the weapons."

A projectile cannon boomed, and a second later, the ship rocked. Katherine smacked her head against the back of her chair. Her fingers flew over the console, and the main glass viewing area around the shuttle shimmered away, the outside becoming a foggy haze. "Energy shields are up."

Clamps unlocked and creaked. The entrance whooshed closed. The shuttle grew quiet. Prasad shook the bolts of the door and said, "All secure, Captain."

Another round of weapons fire shook the ship, though the impact seemed further away, less localized. The putrid scent of melted wires filled Katherine's nostrils.

"Starly, get down to the engine and make sure nothing is on fire," Prasad ordered, slipping into the other command seat. "All clear to take off, Captain."

Katherine set up the auto-launch, and the shuttle groaned and shook as it began its slow lift. Another shot rocked them, and Katherine winced from the pain.

"Son of a bitch," Prasad swore. "They hit our port stabilizer."

"Salim, do you know anything about fixing stabilizers?" Katherine asked, looking over her shoulder.

Salim sat strapped into his chair and said, "Fifteen."

"Huh?"

"Fourteen. Thirteen. Twelve. No, Captain. Eleven."

"What the hell are you doing?" Prasad shouted.

"Eight. Seven. Everyone, heads down and close your eyes. Three."

Katherine shot him a frustrated look, but instinctively, she clenched her muscles and snapped her eyes shut when he reached the end of his countdown. Nothing happened. The shuttle continued to struggle upward, though the affected stabilizer made for an extra-shaky ascent.

"Salim," Katherine said, warning in her tone.

"Huh. I guess you missed, Captain."

White hot pain shot across Katherine's vision when she tried to look over her shoulder at Salim. "Missed what?"

A roaring, metal-crunching sound exploded around them. The shuttle spun upwards against Katherine's commands. Flames erupted around them. Hot, searing flames engulfed the shuttle. The blast glass kept them from being blinded from the light, but even the shields couldn't withstand the heat and crumbled. The shuttle's inside core temperature jumped from the outside temperature of about 3°C to over 40°C in a matter of seconds.

Katherine's stomach rolled, and she vomited coffee all over the console. The gagging, retching sounds around her confirmed she wasn't the only one.

"Hold on everyone," Prasad said in a clear, non-puking voice. "The rollercoaster ride will end in a moment. Salim, what the hell just happened?"

Salim did not answer. Muffin bits exploded from his mouth.

"Ah, shit," Prasad moaned.

Artificial gravity and inertia control balanced to optimum. The shuttle continued up, the autopilot taking control when no command had been given in the last second. Its safety program ensured the ship continued to follow the last order given in case of injury or incapacitation.

Sweat poured down Katherine's face, either from the temperature or from the vomiting.

"What was that?" Katherine shouted.

At the same time, a guard said, "Good shot, Captain."

"It wasn't me!" Katherine looked at Salim and narrowed her eyes.

"It wasn't? I saw a missile tracking them." He shrugged. "Oh well. I suppose that's what happens when you take a bribe from the Coalition. They blow you up and take the cash back."

Katherine's heartbeat pounded in her throat. She looked down. "Um, why is my console covered in blood?"

She was unconscious before she hit the carpeted floor.

CHAPTER TWENTY-FOUR

"Move it! Get out of the way!"

"Patient coming through! Move your ass!"

"Careful! Don't tousle her!"

Katherine wondered why everyone was shouting. It took her two tries before she could ask, "Why is everyone shouting?" The words stuck in her throat. She was dizzy. The world seemed off somehow.

"Captain, can you hear me?"

She blinked and saw Doctor Kramer's smooth face hanging over her. "When did you shave your beard? And why is the ceiling moving?"

"We're rushing you to surgery. You're going to be fine."

Katherine tipped her head to the side. "Why do I need surgery?"

"You've been shot. You have bullet fragments in your thigh, and you have a piece of metal sticking out of your shoulder. We'll have you cleaned up right away. So stay with me, all right?"

Somewhere in the distant reaches of her mind, alarm bells rang. She didn't want them to know that she'd been in a fire-fight. Realizing she'd been caught, and there was no way of getting out of it, Katherine hurled herself upright.

White, searing pain stabbed her, and her vision hazed over

for a moment. The doctor pressed her back against the gurney. "Prasad already explained the training mission. He has some training as a med tech and stopped the bleeding. He saved your life, Captain."

"Training mission?" Katherine asked. Her brain was too slow, too sluggish. "What training mission?"

The doctor looked at her, concerned. "She's in shock. Push it; I need to get this woman into surgery three minutes ago."

Katherine laid her head back on the stretcher, as she was pushed through the open doors of the infirmary. This was it. The lie wouldn't hold. Weapon wounds of any kind were reported. It would be traced. There was no training mission. It was over.

And, even if it wasn't, there was still the badly damaged shuttle that engineering would clearly outline as having been next door to a massive explosion. Oh, and then the Alliance would replay the transmissions that, no doubt, Frum had sent. Even if he didn't, they'd see the wreckage.

Something poked her skin.

How did the ship explode? She didn't remember scoring a direct hit. Or, even a hit. She was busy raising the shields. Salim was at the engine console, blasting power to the thrusters. The weapons were on her console. She didn't hit them.

The world went black as warm fluid entered her veins.

Katherine's eyes popped open. She gasped and sat up, pulling wires and cables with her.

"And, you're awake. Again. I'm getting sick of seeing you in my infirmary. If you keep this up, I'll start to think you've developed a crush on one of my staff."

Katherine did not laugh. She glared at him and said, "Get Salim."

The doctor blinked, startled. Perhaps he expected banter, not a command. She didn't care. Her career was most likely over.

Salim walked in a few seconds after the doctor departed,

clearly having been waiting outside. "Captain, I assumed you'd want to see me when you woke up."

"What did you tell them?" she asked, her voice lowered to a whisper.

"Prasad and I told them we were on a training exercise on Salva when a fuel tank exploded after being hit by weapons fire. We thought it was empty, so it surprised everyone. In the confusion, someone discharged a weapon, probably thought we were under attack, or it might even have happened when several of us were thrown back by the blast."

Katherine swallowed. Salva was in the opposite direction from where they had actually been. Hope blossomed.

"There were, however," Salim said, cautiously, "some transmissions that made it out from Frum's ship before it exploded. I wasn't able to block them all. I'm not certain what got through. It'll take a couple of days before we know."

Katherine's guts clenched. She felt the life drain from her soul. After all she had been through, after everything she'd done, it had been in vain. She had failed.

Salim held up a hand. "Now, Captain, it's too early to fret, and I have every confidence in my abilities. I'm certain I scrambled and garbled their messages so badly that nothing other than the 'the's' and 'we's' got through. But, I felt I should tell you. You might want to work on your alibi and get back to me and the guards."

Katherine stared at him, disgusted. Her alibi? She was days away from being dragged through the station in irons for being a traitor, right after the Alliance declared war on the Union of Planets. "You're kidding? More lies."

He leaned forward, keeping his tone even, but she could hear the strain in it. "Prasad and his guards are Intel, Captain. They know the drill. They had no problem blowing up an Alliance ship and neither should you. They opened fire on us first, after all. Self-defense. We're fine. Fleet Command won't believe the Alliance in any case, if the worst happens. You'll live to fight another day."

"I can't believe what I'm hearing from you. When do the lies stop, Salim? When do I get to go back to who I am?"

"Oh, Captain, the lies never stop. You will never go back to who you were. Never."

Rage billowed inside Katherine. She didn't speak, as she couldn't guarantee what would come out.

"Either way, I think we're lucky," Salim said finally.

"Lucky? Lucky?" she shouted. "You call this fucking lucky?"

He stared at her, his eyes blank. "Yes. Frum was a snake. Even if the documents were real, he wouldn't have done anything with them."

Katherine's mouth dropped. "Then all of this was a waste? I did this for nothing?"

"Not at all," Salim said, offense in his voice. "You are assuming that the transmissions all went through."

"And if they didn't, we still don't have a new ally." She blew out a breath. "Holy shit. I never thought it would come to this. I'll have to turn myself in." Bile rose in her throat.

"You aren't serious?" Salim asked, stepping closer to her.

Katherine raised her hands. "What do you suggest? Waiting around, weaving a list of lies until they catch me? No, I'm an officer of the Fleet. I will take responsibility for my actions. If I do that, perhaps the Alliance won't declare war on us."

He leaned into her personal space. "I will not have you drag me down when we aren't even sure any transmissions have gotten out."

Katherine grabbed his shirt and pulled him even closer, ignoring the stabbing agony in her shoulders. "Are you threatening me?"

"Yes."

"Listen to me, Salim Tobin or whatever in hell's fire your name actually is. You do not threaten me. Ever. Do you hear me? Never threaten me again."

Footsteps sounded, followed by a distinct throat-clearing, Kramer she supposed. Katherine did not let go of Salim, nor did she take her eyes off his.

"Is there a problem?" Kramer asked.

When Katherine didn't hear the footsteps moving away, she growled, "Get. Out." Once she was certain they were alone again, Katherine tightened her grip on Salim. "You have twelve hours to give me proof."

"I need at least two days."

"Twelve hours."

His look was murderous, but he gave her a short nod. "Twelve."

She released him, unable to give him the shove that he deserved. Katherine settled for a grunt of disgust. "Now, get out of here."

Salim gave a long stare at her before turning and walking out of the room.

"Doc, I know you're outside eavesdropping."

The older man stepped into the room, a weary expression on his face. "You all right, Captain?"

"You tell me. I just had surgery."

"There were two fragments, and they came out cleanly. You're going to be sore for a few days, so no training missions." He took a deep breath and exhaled slowly, making no effort to hide his displeasure.

"Thanks. When can I go?"

"Anytime. You need to stay off it for at least a day, to let the sutures take."

Katherine didn't bother to put up a protest. In twelve hours, she'd be turning in her uniform in any case. Too many tiny threads had been left undone. Sooner or later, they'd discover her. She did not want to live her life in hiding, always looking over her shoulder. Instead, she'd wait a few hours to be certain. Then, she'd call Lori and Nova.

And, somehow, she was all right with that.

"I promise to confine myself to quarters until tomorrow."

He raised an eyebrow. "No argument?"

She slid off the bed and picked up her cane. She clapped

a friendly hand on Kramer's shoulder and said, "Thank you."

Kramer narrowed his eyes at her. "What's going on?"

She waved off his concerns. "I need a break, one involving a bottle of two hundred year old Scotch that John left me."

"He was a good man, Katherine." He took a deep breath and said, "You shouldn't mix liquor with your medication."

She didn't reply. Instead, Katherine turned and walked out of the room, heading toward the nearest lift. Mixing booze and meds were the least of her problems. She had twelve hours of freedom left. Patricia wasn't due for at least another day. She would have liked to see her before she surrendered.

CHAPTER TWENTY-FIVE

Katherine slumped against the wall in her kitchenette, clutching a bottle of Scotch older than the Union of Planets. She stared at the golden nectar, swirling it in the glass bottle. Somehow, nearly a third of the bottle had disappeared over the course of the evening. She'd not meant to drink that much. She wouldn't have, either, if she hadn't read the list of the confirmed dead in her family that Sister Mary Nora had sent her.

She'd put off grieving long enough. It was either slip into an emotional breakdown, or get really, really drunk. She picked the latter.

"Computer, voice activation," she slurred.

"Voice activated," the computer replied, still sounding annoyingly like O'Connor.

"Dim lights fifty percent."

The lights dimmed, though not enough to take the edge off her growing headache.

"Another fifty percent."

Shadowed darkness fell over her quarters. "Better," she mumbled to herself before turning off the voice activation.

The liquor calmed the anguish, at least. Or, perhaps it only delayed the inevitable. It had been good of John to leave her his entire collection of wines and spirits. Hopefully, Security wouldn't confiscate everything when the time came. Maybe she could convince Lori to keep the quarters available for Patricia. She'd like to make sure that someone got to enjoy John's life collection.

John. Her best friend in the world, shot in the head during a riot because she was in a coma. Could she have prevented it, or would it have been her dust to get dumped into space?

Tears streamed down Katherine's face, though no sounds escaped her. It was too hard to sob. The hurt was too much. She tried so hard. She did everything in her power and nothing. *Nothing.*

"Incoming message from Salim Tobin."

"Voice only. I assume the answer is no," she said. Or, at least, that's what she thought she said.

"What did you say?"

"I said I assume the answer is no," she said slower, focusing on each individual word.

An annoyed sigh came from the other end. "Captain, you're drunk."

"Yup," she said. "Shoosh, don't tell anyone. I got into John's fine Scotch."

"Surely you aren't going to turn yourself in like this?"

Katherine shook her head and then remembered that she had only voice on. "No. In the morning, when I wake up."

"Captain, I really want you to wait. I'm not certain, but I believe the Alliance thinks—"

"I don't care, Salim," Katherine said. "It's over. Even if the transmission didn't get through, they'll find Frum's ship. It'll get pieced together. Hang me now, hang me later."

He took a deep breath before saying, "I regret what I said in the hospital."

"I don't. Francis out." The communications system beeped, severing the connection.

She went back to resting her head against the wall, eyes closed, consciousness fading.

"Incoming call, Landing Pad Seven."

Katherine's eyes shot open. Dazed, she looked around. Still sitting up, bottle wedged between her thighs, she must have fallen asleep.

"Ignore." She stared at the bottle and slurred, "Why would I have a call from Landing Pad Seven? Wrong fucking number. I'm all alone. Just me and you left in the universe."

"Incoming call, OPs."

"Ignore," she ordered. Once she had arrived in her quarters, she'd called Lori and advised her that she was going to get some sleep and didn't want to be disturbed. The logical, command part of her told her to answer, that it could be about the war. If it had been, she was in no state to look after it. In a few hours, she'd have nothing more to do with the war. Let Lori get the practice now.

"Incoming call, OPs."

"Ignore," Katherine snapped. "Turn off incoming communications."

"Communications disabled."

Katherine eased herself to the floor, dragging herself to where a small rug lay. She rested her cheek on it, the remainder of her body still on the metal floor. She faded out into visions of Randall White bleeding to death over and over. The blood wouldn't come off her hands.

After several nightmares, the door chime woke her. She ignored it. Even if she wanted to answer it, which she didn't, Katherine wasn't convinced she could even crawl to the door. For the first time in her life, she truly understood why people became addicts; there was great comfort in having raw emotion dulled and blunted. It would be easy to get used to.

The door chimed again, its shrill insistence drilling a hole in her head.

"Go away," Katherine attempt to shout, though it sounded more slurred.

The key lock beeped as numbers were punched in. She clutched her bottle tighter. "Go away."

She wanted to enjoy her last night of freedom. In the morning, she would turn herself in to Lori, to be labeled a traitor responsible for billions of deaths as the combined force of the Coalition and the Alliance swept across the Union territory. No one would care that she had been trying to help.

"Leave me the hell alone."

Metal doors slid open, and the warm air from the corridor slammed into the room. There, standing on the threshold, was a vision of humanity.

Patricia.

She had lost weight, her clothing hung too loosely off her body. Her face was haggard, tanned, with bits of pink from sunburns in the process of healing. Katherine wanted to say something glib, something non-committal, but she could not. Any words would break her. She wished for Patricia not to speak, yet longed to hear her voice.

"This explains why you didn't meet me on the docking ring," Patricia said, her voice frustrated. Angry, even.

Katherine felt even more of a failure. That's why Patricia left her to begin with. The job was more important than their marriage. It was again today. The job came before Patricia. She pulled herself up to a sitting position, the room spinning on its axis. Her stomach rolled. "I didn't know."

Patricia crossed her arms. "You might've if you weren't pissed drunk on the floor, ignoring my calls. What a mess you are."

Katherine tried to make an angry comment. She really tried. "I—" Her voice hitched. A short sob, a gasp of emotion, replaced the words. Katherine clawed at the floor, failing to hold back her grief, her pain, her agony any longer.

It was too much. "Oh God, Patricia. What have I done?" Katherine collapsed to the floor, sobbing, her glass bottle clanging against the steel floor. Golden liquid splashed out of the bottle, spreading like White's blood from his chest. She gasped, hiccupped, sobbed.

Billions would die. Because of her. Because she failed.

Strong, familiar arms wrapped around Katherine, pulling her aching, exhausted body upright. "Oh, Kat, it'll be all right," Patricia cooed, her voice soft and gentle.

It made Katherine hurt more. "No, it won't be. You don't understand what I've done."

Patricia took a deep breath. "Then tell me."

Out of habit, Katherine snapped back, "I can't." Then, it dawned on her that everyone would know in the next twenty-four hours. She needed to decide if she wanted to tell her wife first, or have her learn about it on the news Net. She sighed. "Everyone will know soon enough."

Katherine told her. Patricia remained silent as Katherine recounted the entire tale. She stroked her hair. When she was done, Katherine looked up at her. "You can leave now. I'll sign the divorce papers. I won't fight you."

Patricia's eyebrows pulled together. "I don't follow."

"You sent me divorce papers a month ago. I haven't signed them. I was going to call but never got around to it." Katherine licked her lips. "I suppose it doesn't matter now. I won't be much good to you in a maximum penal colony." Katherine's voice quavered. "For the rest of my life."

"Shh," Patricia whispered. "I'm not going anywhere."

Katherine pulled herself up and stared at her wife. "I have to turn myself in."

Patricia nodded. "I agree. They will go easier on you that way."

"They're going to send me to prison."

Patricia nodded. "Yes, they will. We can fight it, though. I refuse to have you labeled a traitor for trying to end the war. Stupid, yes. Foolhardy, definitely. Traitor? No. I don't accept that."

Katherine swatted at her face, trying to clear the tears from her eyes. The dread inside her did not leave, but it lifted a little. "Will you stay with me tonight?"

Patricia nodded. "I'll go with you to Lori in the morning."

Katherine put her head back down and said, “I thought I could save us all. How arrogant.”

Patricia kissed the top of her head. “I would call it brave. Your family would have been proud that you tried.”

The alcohol and pain and grief pulled at Katherine’s consciousness. She faded away, thinking there were worse ways to spend her last moments of freedom.

CHAPTER TWENTY-SIX

Someone relentless leaned on the buzzer, forcing Katherine to open her eyes. She was in bed, with no memory how she got there.

"Baby, I think they're here."

Katherine closed her eyes and opened them again. A warm comfort spread through her. Patricia had not been a dream. Soft lips kissed her bare shoulder. "Go shower. You smell. I'll hold them off."

Katherine's stomach rolled, partially from John's Scotch and partially from the sinking, horrific feeling of defeat. She had lost.

Katherine forced open her eyes to watch Patricia slink out of bed naked and pull on the fleece robe from the floor. A tinge of guilt hit Katherine. She thought she was without family. She had never expected Patricia to come back. Now, here at the end, she discovered they had only argued, the way old married couples do. Katherine's stubbornness was what had sent her away.

She hauled herself from the warmth of the bed to stare at her reflection in the mirror. She looked awful with the haggard look of someone rather drunk. No doubt she still smelled like it, too. Katherine groaned when she turned up the brightness of the lights, her eyes and head both protesting.

The muted voices from the other room gained intensity. She couldn't pick out the entire conversation but could hear Patricia's strong voice insisting that they wait for Katherine to shower.

"What?" Patricia exclaimed, the surprise and shock audible even through the walls.

Katherine's ears perked up at that. She grabbed the electric toothbrush and dragged it across her teeth without turning it on. Still in her robe, she headed into the living room to discover Lori, no surprise there. But next to her stood Jayson Williams. Why on earth would the head of tactical be there? Shouldn't Ambrose have come, being in charge of security?

Katherine's stomach clenched, forcing bile upwards. She swallowed it back down, choking. "Good morning."

Williams inclined his head. "Captain, we need to go. Now."

Katherine cleared her throat, straightening her shoulders. "Yes, well, if you don't mind, I would like to shower and change into a clean uniform first. I'm sure Fleet Command will allow me that dignity before—"

Patricia grabbed her arm. Hard. "The Alliance declared war on the Coalition."

"What?" Katherine whispered. Her knees buckled beneath her. Lori and Patricia grabbed an arm each, keeping her upright.

"Captain, you all right?" Williams asked.

The room tipped, exactly as it had when the news first came that Pious III had been invaded. She had done it. She had brought the Alliance into the war. They were going to win. They would beat back the tide of death. She'd saved them. She had saved them all.

"Captain?" Williams asked, waving a hand in front of her face.

"Katherine? Katherine, can you hear me?" Patricia asked frantically.

All the lies, the deception, what she had done to Raewadee, killing White, killing Frum...it was worth it.

The Alliance had entered the war. She survived. Her career

survived.

She did it.

"Sorry, Lori, she took too much pain medicine last night. She's still off balance."

Williams snorted. "She smells like she took a bath in liquor." He looked at Lori. "You said she was on medical orders for the night."

Lori shrugged. "She was off-duty. How was I supposed to know the Alliance would join the war with her still drunk?"

Katherine started laughing, first a short snort followed by a bellowing, roaring laugh that wouldn't stop. Salim had killed the transmission! They'd done it.

"Okay, Katherine, you gotta sober up," Patricia said sternly. "Now."

"Aye, aye, wife," Katherine said with a sloppy salute. She stopped her laughing, though the smile stayed plastered on her face. "Let me get dressed, Lori. And get me some coffee."

Katherine staggered to the bathroom, near skipping. She didn't know why the Alliance entered the war, and she didn't care. They had done it. Somehow, the entire scheme failed, and yet, they had done it.

Horror spread through Katherine. "Ambrose, you're joking."

The security chief shook her head. "I'm quite serious. A minor Alliance representative named Arthur Frum discovered the Coalition planned to assassinate key members of his government. He was bribed with several million credits to keep silent about it but then sent the information to his government anyway. He was pursued by the Coalition and, apparently, detoured toward Perdition for our protection. His ship was destroyed before he reached here."

Katherine's mouth hung open. This was not how things unfolded. How could the Alliance fabricate such a tale from a burned wreck?

"The Alliance asked Fleet Command for permission to enter our space to investigate, which was granted several hours ago. They found data pads, a holo-vid, and several computer entries. They were incomplete, but most of the information survived the explosion. It appears that the representative had put everything in a blast-resistant container with a beacon, and he ejected it before being destroyed. The Alliance declared war twenty minutes ago. Two hundred attack ships have already crossed into Union territory to begin fortifying our key facilities while they prepare for mobilization."

"We're talking thousands of ships," Williams said, whistling. "The tide has turned."

"Captain, are you all right?" Windrunner asked.

Katherine looked at Lori then to the others. Her heart sped up, and she struggled to breathe. "I don't understand."

Her senior officers stared at her. She imagined that they could all smell the stale liquor on her; she could even smell it. No doubt, they thought she was drunk, which she was, and unable to follow, which she wasn't. "I understand the words you're saying. They simply don't make sense to me."

"Most things don't make sense in war, Captain," Raewadee said, looking away as she spoke, her face still covered in bandages and film.

Katherine gritted her teeth. She turned to Lori and asked, "Then it's official? The Alliance has joined the war?"

Lori nodded, a wide smile on her face. "Yes. The Seventh Fleet is heading to Destiny Station to sign the official treaty as we speak. John would have been so happy."

Katherine nodded, though she couldn't follow. Why didn't the Alliance ship send out a distress message? Why didn't they get word back to their government? She couldn't understand why the Alliance had not declared war on them. *Salim.*

"Captain?" Nova asked.

Katherine snapped her attention to Nova. She had not realized that she'd spoken Salim's name out loud.

"Excuse me, I'm not feeling well. Lori, please handle the

remainder and update me later."

Katherine staggered out of the meeting, toward a lift. She needed answers. She was going to get them, even if she had to drag them out of Salim.

CHAPTER TWENTY-SEVEN

"What a pleasant surprise," Salim said as he unlocked his security gate across his shop front. "What can I do for you?"

Katherine glared at Salim and forced out, "Inside. Now."

He blinked in surprise but inclined his head and motioned for her to step in. Once inside, he latched the door, which re-tinted the windows dark. "I assume you're here to tell me the news about the Alliance joining our good cause."

It might have been the arrogant smile on his face, or perhaps it was the lingering effects of the Scotch in her system, but something within her snapped. She grabbed a purse stand and swung it at Salim, cracking him in the ribs. He hadn't been prepared for the assault and fell against a table of bicarbonate-based bath spheres. The table, Salim, and the nuclear dust bombs crashed to the floor. A mushroom cloud of floral-scented particles rose from the heap.

"Was that really necessary?" he shouted as he struggled to his feet.

Anger bubbled inside her. "You were the one who blew up their ship!"

His expression morphed into one of self-important satisfaction. "Yes."

Her entire body shook, and she clenched her fists in a futile attempt to control the adrenaline rush. "You were going to murder Frum all along."

"Yes. The container that held the data chips also held a small explosive device. When it got near the ship, it attached to the outer hull wall."

She grabbed another metal stand, but Salim was ready for the blow this time. He grabbed the metal pole mid-swing and pushed against her but not enough to knock her over. He managed to pull it from her and tossed it behind him. The clang of metal against the tiled floor scraped at Katherine's nerves.

"How could you?" she whispered. "You murdered them."

Salim examined her face for a moment before laughing. "You hypocrite."

"I beg your pardon?"

"You heard me. Shall I recount your transgressions? Let's see. Murder, impeding the lawful investigation of a crime, human trade, dealing in weapons. Did I miss anything?"

"I never wanted anyone to die," she snarled.

He snorted. "Then, why did you approach me of all people? Was it my warm and fuzzy reputation, or because you knew I could do the things your perfect little world couldn't handle?"

Katherine glared at him as a trickle of doubt penetrated her rage. Why *did* she ask Salim for his help? Why did she so easily fall into the murky grey waters of morality?

She wanted to end the war.

"I never wanted Frum or his guards to die." Her voice was quiet now. "Killing him was in self-defense."

Unlike with Randall White, her conscience whispered.

"You killed him because he caught you. You could have run inside the ship, tuck-tail and fled, but you shot him. You killed him."

A lump formed in Katherine's throat, and she struggled to breathe. He was right. She held back the urge to vomit. She was a murderer, just as Salim was.

Just like White.

"Let's not forget poor Second Lieutenant Bindu Raewadee,

either. Oh, no, we can't forget her. Bringing Randall White to the station was bad enough, but you didn't have strong enough security, and he broke out. He attacked me, Prasad, and all those fine, fine Intel guards. He beat Raewadee, burned her, and would have raped her if you'd given him the chance. And what did you do, Captain? How did you comfort that young woman in her time of need?"

Katherine swallowed. Her voice came out bitter, harsh. "I threatened to ruin her if she didn't allow the investigation to close."

He showed his palms. "There you have it. You're little more than a rapist and a murderer yourself. Yet, you come in here all self-righteous, when you are an immoral criminal like the rest of us. You sacrificed your morals and beliefs for the greater good."

She stiffened. "What does that make you?"

"Oh, a criminal. I was an assassin for a good portion of my adult life and part of my teens, as well. At least, I admit that fact. What is your excuse? Hiding behind that grey uniform, hoping no one notices what a pale shadow of morality you've become?"

Katherine averted her eyes. She didn't want to even see her own reflection in the mirrors behind him.

"Cheer up, Captain. You'll grow a thicker skin soon enough. And if your conscience does start bothering you, remember you saved the entire Union of Planets on a blue light special. Your superiors will sing your praises, Intel will probably recruit you, and the mothers and fathers whose children are not killed in this conflict will eternally thank you."

Katherine turned and headed out of the store. She wanted nothing more to do with him. Looking at him was like looking in the mirror, and she wanted no part of that right now.

She was a killer. She brought the Alliance into the war by dirtying her hands so badly that they would never come clean.

And yet, she'd do it again. That was the damning thing about it all. She'd do it all over again.

CHAPTER TWENTY-EIGHT

Katherine stared at the hazy image of Admiral Ortora cutting in and out over the secure communications channel. She struggled against rubbing her eyes and yawning. Words could not describe her exhaustion.

"I understand that Perdition's been made headquarters for the Alliance's Third Fleet," Sam said with an unusual amount of pep in her voice.

"Yes, they have," Katherine said, not bothering to hide either her irritation or exhaustion. The time for her to have celebrated the entry of the Alliance into the war was long past. Since it joined the war effort a week ago, she'd been running on next to no sleep.

Sam raised her eyebrows expectantly.

Katherine took a deep breath to control her frustration. It wasn't Sam's fault. She was beyond tired. "The Third Fleet has agreed to share some of the workload. As soon as they are trained up on our processes, Perdition staff will begin an R & R rotation. Some of the senior staff haven't had time off in months. We're at the stage where the doc is threatening to mass suspend everyone from active duty."

Sam nodded before narrowing her eyes. "When was the last time you had more than twelve hours off?"

"When I was in the coma," Katherine said bitterly.

Sam licked her lips. Or, at least it seemed like that, with the screen blinking in and out. "How is the pain? Is it getting better?"

Katherine frowned. "Right now, the only pain I have is Doc Kramer nagging at me to take time off so that I'll heal faster."

Sam cocked her head.

"Don't give me that look. You have no idea what I've gone through the past several weeks." More bitterness dripped into her tone than she had meant.

There was a pause. "Mission accomplished?"

Katherine considered not answering. It seemed a rather stupid question, really. "Isn't it rather obvious?"

"Good work."

"I can't look at myself in the mirror anymore," Katherine grunted, "but I suppose that's a small price for the safety of the Union."

"Patricia messaged me this morning." Sam looked down at something. "I'm glad you're back together. Your marriage is the only one I've stood up at that hasn't ended in divorce. Patricia said she's still with—"

"Doctors without brains? Yeah, she's still with them. The stubborn wench leaves for the front lines in two weeks. She's helping the Alliance set up a field hospital. At least she won't be nagging me to take better care of myself." Katherine didn't want her to go, but arguing with Patricia about her job was as useless as arguing with, well, herself. Both of them were stubborn mules. That's why they got along so well.

"I've sent Commander Windrunner a change to your orders." Sam looked up at her, a faint smile curled the corners of her mouth. "Effective immediately, you are on medical leave for a month."

Katherine blinked. A month? She'd not had that much time off since high school. "Sam, look, I don't need your charity."

"No, but you do need someone to tie you to a chair and take away your computer access." She looked down at her console again. "I have requested that Windrunner restrict your computer access starting tomorrow, to prevent you from working during your leave. She will look after the Alliance's needs until then."

Katherine hesitated. No computer access?

Sam leaned forward. "She can handle it, right?"

"Oh, absolutely. No question at all." Katherine looked over the monitor screen out at Lori in OPs. "I had gotten used to the notion of doing it myself, that's all."

"Too bad. You're off duty. I suggest you clean up your office before she gets the message."

Katherine was too weary to argue. She had never felt so bruised in her life. Not her body, but her soul, her confidence. "Fine."

"Good work, Kat."

Katherine inclined her head and ended the transmission. Was this the end of her friendship with Sam? How could she overcome the guilt for what she'd done, in the face of Sam's request? Would Sam forgive her if she'd known what Katherine had done?

Before Katherine could call Lori, her office doors whooshed open. Her heart sank as a sullen, weary young woman walked into her office. The inevitable could never be put off. "Good morning, Lieutenant."

"Captain," she said without expression, though her eyes were filled with hatred. "You requested to see me."

"Yes, please sit down."

Raewadee remained standing.

Katherine cleared her throat but did not repeat the offer. "I called you because I wanted to know if you had considered your options."

"Regarding me leaving?"

"Yes."

Raewadee stared at her for a moment. Katherine folded her hands on her desk, letting the woman form her thoughts. She could give her that, at least. "Why was Randall White on the station?"

Katherine's insides tightened. "That's classified."

"I want to know, Captain. It's not in any official records. Everything about him leads back to you. I want to know why. "

"I told you, it's classified." Katherine took a deep breath. "Why do you want to know?"

Raewadee flinched at her tone. She shifted her eyes around the room, not wanting to focus on Katherine. "I haven't known you very long, but everyone speaks of you like you're this beacon of morality. You can do no wrong. I can't figure out why you would make me drop..." Her voice hitched. "After what he did to me. I should be allowed to know why he was here. You wouldn't even do that for me."

"I am sorry for what happened to you. Truly, I am. But, there are more important things than you being violated. If you can't handle that, then I suggest you don't re-enlist when your term comes up. Or, perhaps you can refuse to work and spend the next couple of years on a penal colony. Either way, you are a Fleet Officer. You should understand that duty is first."

"Getting burned and assaulted wasn't part of my duty."

Katherine stood. She slammed her hands on her desk and snapped, "It was. My lie saved millions of lives. Preserving your faith in me is worthless in the face of that. Your *life* is worthless against that outcome. And if I had it to do all over again, I'd do it again and again and again."

Raewadee's eyes glistened.

Katherine controlled her tone, even if the adrenaline throbbed in her veins. "You will never know why he was on the station, and you will never know why I lied. What you can know, however, is that I was doing my duty to the entire Union of Planets. Your ability to sleep at night and my ability to look in the mirror is a rather small price to pay."

Raewadee gave Katherine a dubious stare. "*Your* ability?"

Katherine licked her lips, finding herself somewhere between sympathy and annoyance. She had not meant for Raewadee to be assaulted. It wasn't as though it was a part of the agenda. She worked to harden her own heart against the things she had done and a small part of her resented that Raewadee couldn't do the same.

Or, more accurately, that Raewadee's ethics were still too pure to be heated, melded, changed.

"I will not apologize for being human and lacking the ability to see the future." Katherine stood away from her desk. "Now, I have been placed on medical leave for the next month, and I have a lot to do. Either make your decision, or I will make it for you."

Katherine tapped at her console, transferring documents to her personal account, in case she wanted to do a little work back in her quarters. What Admiral Ortora didn't know wouldn't hurt her. It wasn't like Patricia would let her work much while she was still on the station.

She looked up, surprised to see that Raewadee had not left her office. Katherine raised an eyebrow at the young woman.

"I want to stay on Perdition, Captain." Her voice was meek, diffident.

Katherine narrowed her eyes at her. "Are you sure?"

"Yes," Raewadee said, raising her chin in an indignant stance. "I want to be removed from Command, however. I don't want to be a career officer any longer. I'd rather focus on being an engineer."

Katherine gave a stiff nod. She'd have to call in significant favors to remove Raewadee from officer ranks during a war, even if the Alliance had turned the tide. She'd get it done. "It will take time. Submit the transfer request, and I'll have Commander Windrunner start looking for a replacement. You'll be responsible for training the person."

Raewadee didn't answer. She merely lowered her eyes before turning to walk out. Katherine had planned to let her go, but the words slipped out before her brain could stop her. "Raewadee, wait."

The young woman did not turn around, but she froze in her tracks.

"I regret you lost faith in me. I never meant to hurt you,

directly or otherwise."

Raewadee's shoulders trembled a little before she walked up to the sliding doors, pressed the side panel, and walked out before the doors finished opening.

Katherine sank back into her chair, wincing against the stinging wound in her thigh. At least the dull ache that still existed over most of her body was slowly subsiding. Soon, she'd feel like her old self. At least, her old physical self. She doubted she'd ever feel like her old self ever again.

Her number of messages updated at the bottom of the screen. Idly, she read the most recent one, a summary casualty report. In a matter of a week, their death toll had dropped by 322%. The Alliance did that.

Chills spread through her body. She had done that. Millions were alive. Because of her. Because she had succeeded.

Realization dawned on her. It didn't matter, in the end, how she felt. What mattered was that she succeeded.

Katherine tapped her communications panel. "Commander, I need you."

Only a moment passed before Lori entered. "Yes, Captain."

Katherine had considered working for an extra couple of days on the sly, helping Lori transition. But, when she looked at the rejuvenated second-in-command, she smiled. A little adversity was just what the crew needed, or else they'd get a little soft in this new age of Alliance-Union friendship.

"Admiral Ortora has forced me to take a month off. So, it looks like you're in charge."

Lori's mouth dropped. "You're kidding! Did she threaten you?"

Katherine beamed. "Remember to water my plants. And keep your feet off my desk."

Katherine walked out of the room, enjoying the rare moment of lightness she felt in her step. She could eventually learn to like herself again. And, even if she didn't, it was rather a small price to pay for victory.

ABOUT THE AUTHOR

Krista D. Ball is a Canadian speculative fiction author who is currently hiding from necromancers. Better safe than undead.

Coming soon from Mundania Press
Also by Krista D. Ball

TRANQUILITY S BLAZE

Just as Lady Bethany settles into the comfortable routine of her life, her magic-addicted twin sister emerges from exile to usurp the Gentle Goddess, Apexia; their own mother. To stop her, Bethany must choose between her duty to destiny and her desire for freedom. Either way, her choice will cost her more than she is willing to pay.

Spring, 2012